FRAMED IN GUILT

William Barridge, meek and mild solicitor's clerk, is found lying on the floor of his employer's locked office with a knife in his back. But how could a man so innocuous have had any enemies . . . ? When Superintendent Henshaw investigates, however, it becomes evident that Barridge had mysterious dealings with his brother in Australia — and an association with an attractive potential divorcee. Added to the list of suspects is Henry Minton, Barridge's employer — the only person with a key to the locked office . . .

JOHN RUSSELL FEARN

FRAMED
IN GUILT

Complete and Unabridged

LINFORD
Leicester

First published in Great Britain

First Linford Edition
published 2007

British Library CIP Data

Fearn, John Russell, *1908 – 1960*
    Framed in guilt.—Large print ed.—
Linford mystery library
    1. Murder—Investigation—Fiction
    2. Detective and mystery stories
    3. Large type books
    I. Title
    823.9'12 [F]

    ISBN 978–1–84617–640–1

Published by
F. A. Thorpe (Publishing)
Anstey, Leicestershire
Set by Words & Graphics Ltd.
Anstey, Leicestershire
Printed and bound in Great Britain by
T. J. International Ltd., Padstow, Cornwall

This book is printed on acid-free paper

1

William Barridge was convinced that the telephone was ringing in his office. Louder and louder still it rang, and in desperation he lunged out with his hand. Somebody shrieked. He opened an eye and stared at a gray pinnacle looming before him.

'You idiot! You nearly poked my eye out!'

Barridge smiled tiredly and relaxed. The 'telephone' was the savage little alarm clock on the bedside table; the 'pinnacle' the window of the bedroom, glazed with February frost, the curtains closed at the top and open slightly at the bottom, allowing light to shine through basc and apex.

It was Monday, February 3. Not just the start of another week — but a Monday to which William Barridge had been looking forward. He tried to muse on this fact but the 'telephone' at which he had lunged went on with her muttered protests.

'William! What *ails* you?'

'I . . . I was dreaming,' Barridge said half to himself.

'Huh! These days you never do anything else! And what about my cup of tea? I can't start a hard day's work without something to stir my circulation. It's gone seven o'clock!'

Barridge rose up in bed and shuddered. Muttering remarks about the inclemency of the British winter, he scrambled out of bed and bundled on his dressing gown. Rubbing his thinning hair he drove his feet into icy slippers and stumbled to the window, flinging back the curtains with a grating rasp.

'*Must* you make that noise?' his wife demanded.

'The curtains have to be put back, dear. I think we could do with some grease on the runners.'

'That's it! Complain about the way I've fixed the curtains!'

'I didn't mean it in that sense,' William Barridge said mildly, as he went to the door.

In winter, this modern semi-detached

villa in Hadlam, a small but thriving Midlands town, was the nearest thing to a vault Barridge had ever experienced. He went along the short upper landing, past the doors where his noisy offspring were still asleep, and then down the narrow staircase.

Ice was thick on the windows.

He was blowing on his hands by the time he reached the gas stove in the kitchen and filled the kettle with water. The gas stove ring exploded violently as the match was applied and William Barridge scowled. He could still smell the lingering odour of unlighted gas: his sense of smell was uncannily keen. Sometimes it had proven a useful gift: sometimes decidedly not.

'Monday . . . ' he muttered. 'That's good . . . '

He pondered, a forlorn-looking figure in his worn dressing gown, his greying hair struggling for survival on his head. He was narrow-shouldered, stood five feet seven, and had an unhealthy pallor. No Adonis, he had thin cheeks, a long, straight nose, a fairly high forehead, and a disproportionate, loose-lipped mouth. His eyes were pale grey, below sandy, wispy brows utterly out of keeping with his grey hair. He was forty-four, but looked a good twenty years older.

Sober, quiet, married now for twenty years, having three obstreperous children ranging from twelve years to sixteen, paying for his villa on the never-never system, owning a car which refused to go in winter time, and holding down one job at one salary because he had neither the wit nor the courage to attempt anything better.

He realized suddenly that the water was boiling. He put three spoonfuls of tea into the pot and poured water into it. With equal care he pulled the thick, hideous-looking cosy into position. Finally he took cups and saucers from the cupboard, filled two, added sugar and milk, and carried them up to the bedroom.

Emily Barridge was sitting up waiting for him, an old bed jacket round her lumpy shoulders. 'Thought you'd gone to sleep down there,' she commented.

'Sorry, dear — the water took rather

long to heat. I expect the gas pressure's down.'

His wife accepted the teacup with ill grace. Barridge sat on the edge of the bed and sipped his own tea noiselessly, his pale gray eyes on his wife's face.

The daughter of a provision merchant, she had once fascinated him with her auburn hair and bright blue eyes. She been slim then, bright — even vivacious. Now she had put on flesh and acquired laziness at the same time. She was not far short of being really fat. The auburn hair was streaked with grey, the sensitive features coarsened, the mouth pulled down at the corners.

'What are you staring at, William? I can't help the way I look! I'd soon look very different if you'd get a decent job and decent money. What good has Minton ever done you?'

'There might be worse employers than Minton.'

'There couldn't be! He does nothing but take advantage of you. Besides, he drinks, and that's quite enough for me! I don't trust anybody who drinks.'

Barridge shrugged. He had heard it all before.

'For heaven's sake, why don't you stand up for yourself and demand something better?'

'I can't.' Barridge put his teacup gently on the table beside the bed. 'Being head clerk to a solicitor is about as high as I can get since I haven't passed the necessary examinations to become a solicitor . . . I don't do too badly.'

'Maybe *you* don't, but *I* do! I've the house and three children to look after. We're getting no younger, William. It's time we had a maid — or help of some sort. And that needs money.'

'You'll have it one day, my dear . . . when I'm dead.' He smiled cynically. 'I'm well insured,' he added. 'And my health isn't all that it might be.'

'Nothing wrong with you!' his wife declared flatly. 'Unless it's self-pity — '

'None of us can tell when we're going to die, Emily. I'm sure I shall die suddenly when it does come.' William Barridge smiled enigmatically. He rose to his feet. 'I think I'd better be getting dressed.'

As he went along the short landing he knocked hard on the two neighbouring doors and received muttered sleepy grumbles from Harold, Basil, and Lucy respectively. Once the children were thoroughly awake he was, as he well knew, at their mercy.

He went down into the kitchen again, poured the remains of the kettle's hot water into a jug and took it up to the bathroom. Here he stood shuddering whilst he shaved. The blade was under the weather and snicked the top off a spot on the side of his jaw.

'Shan't need to worry about you again, anyway,' he murmured, and snatched up the styptic pencil.

Ablution completed, he returned towards the bedroom to dress, pausing to listen at the head of the stairs. Basil, the eldest boy, was busy at his daily job — lighting the fire before dressing himself. Barridge went on into his bedroom and, still shivering, began to dress. Near the bed his wife was doing likewise, but neither of them exchanged any words.

So towards eight o'clock they both

went down into the kitchen for breakfast, the fire crackling noisily and smokily. Emily Barridge began to prepare something on the gas-cooker, and her husband glanced through the morning paper. A tuft of cotton wool projected from his jaw where the uneven razorblade had done its work.

'I suppose it doesn't occur to you to help get breakfast?' his wife snapped. 'All you do is sit there in your black coat and striped trousers, as if you were the Lord of the manor!'

Barridge sighed, then put the newspaper aside. His wife noticed the page he had been studying as it fell face upwards on the table.

'Racing!' she exclaimed in scorn. 'Sheer waste of time! You never gambled in your life. In fact you never did anything except rush up and down for Mr. Minton. The most exciting thing you ever do is write to that brother of yours in Australia.' Mrs. Barridge heaved a reflective sigh.

'Now there's a real man!' she declared. 'Made his way in a strange country — and his pile. Not like you!'

Bacon, what there was of it, fizzled noisily as she shimmied the pan over the grilling ring. Barridge said nothing. He commenced setting the table — then he went no farther as the juvenile earthquake from upstairs struck the kitchen.

Lucy, Basil, and Harold all began talking at once, about nothing in particular. Barridge returned to his chair and newspaper. He remained absorbed in it when his share of the breakfast arrived. There was peace, of a kind. His wife was so involved with handling the children she had no time for anything else. Barridge ate his meagre breakfast, casting his eye at the same time over the events of the outer world.

By eight-thirty breakfast was over and one by one the children departed to school. Since there exists in the young mind an eternal tendency to hero-worship, it said much for the children's opinion of their father that they only bade him a cursory 'Goodbye, Dad . . . ' whereas their mother was considered worth a kiss and a hug.

The front door banged behind the last

of the trio. Barridge laid the paper on one side. He took out his watch and glanced at it, checking it by the clock on the mantelshelf.

'That clock's five minutes slow,' he announced.

'Not the only thing ... ' Emily Barridge sat half hunched at the untidy table, considering him. 'Oh, William, I do wish you'd wake up and do something! There are times when I even feel like ending it all.'

Her husband smiled mirthlessly. 'Your sort don't do that, Emily. It takes courage,' and before she could absorb the insult he went on: 'I can't change my occupation and profession at my time of life. You have a roof over your head, three healthy children, and enough money to get by. What more do you want?'

'A lot more. The struggle and monotony are killing me. And you're so — so horribly meek about everything! I know the Bible says that the meek shall inherit the earth, but you've proved it wrong!'

Barridge merely shrugged.

'That's it!' his wife snapped. 'You can't

defend yourself, can you? You've done nothing but lick boots ever since I've known you. I — I thought when we married that you'd get out of it. I'm left wondering how much longer it's going to go on.'

'I can't change my nature,' Barridge answered flatly. 'I've always been taken advantage of, ever since being a boy. I spent all my adolescence being kicked around by one and another — Yes, even by girls. Metaphorically, of course. They made me look a fool after leading me up the garden path. I — I didn't forget them for it, though,' he went on, with a tightening of his loose mouth. 'I never do forget things like that. I think perhaps . . . ' Barridge swallowed the last mouthful of tepid tea, 'my health may have something to do with it.'

'So you're blaming *that* again, are you? That's no excuse, William. Except for that time when you had rheumatism you've been up and around every day of your life.'

'Just the same I don't feel well.' He got to his feet. 'And haven't done for long enough — Is my lunch made up?' he asked, changing the subject as he glanced round the table.

His wife picked up a small brown paper package tied with string plentifully adorned with knots. In the package, he knew, would be three cheese sandwiches. He would dearly have loved to have the dinner at home in the middle of the day — if only to break the monotony of office life — but Emily refused to prepare it. With the three children getting their mid-day meals at the school she saw no reason to step out of line to prepare something for her husband alone. Evening was soon enough for all of them. There had been a time, certainly, when she had always prepared a hot meal at noon and had been waiting, spruce and tidy with her hair brushed and a clean apron on, for the arrival of her brand-new husband. That had been long ago, though.

'Thanks.' Barridge put the package in his jacket pocket. Then he went out into the hall and donned topcoat and bowler hat, put an umbrella over his arm from sheer force of habit.

'You'll be back at six?' his wife asked him, almost filling the kitchen door frame.

'Yes, dear — six as usual. Good bye.'

Barridge stepped out into the frosty grey of the February morning. Ten years ago he had never failed to kiss his wife goodbye. Today it was probably the thing remotest from his mind . . .

2

Usually Barridge went straight to his office in Parkhurst Street, arriving there at 9.15, half an hour before his boss, Henry Minton. This morning, instead of getting on the No. 11 'bus which would have dropped him nearby, he took a No. 6 to the town centre and alighted several stops before Parkhurst Street.

He walked along the pavement, unheeding and unheeded by commuters surging to and fro. He walked for perhaps another quarter of a mile, and then stopped at the end of a street. At the far end of it was a garish facade with eighteen-inch letters across it proclaiming AMUSEMENT ARCADE.

Behind it was a covered market sporting all kinds of stores — chiefly vegetable and foodstuffs, mixed promiscuously with amusement machines. Beyond the arcade the street continued and led into the heart of the town and the top of

Parkhurst Street. Barridge had been through the arcade numberless times and speculated upon its various offerings — but this time he had an object in view.

Ten minutes later he emerged on the other side, walking swiftly now and carrying in one hand a circular object in brown paper, sealed with gum-strip. Instead of going to his office he went to the nearest stationer's and bought a sheet of stiff brown paper, some corrugated cardboard, and a small ball of twine.

His next call was at the general post office, where he carefully wrapped it into a neat circular shape in the brown paper and finally tied it firmly with string. From his pocket he took a small lump of red sealing wax, struck a match, and sealed down the knots.

He carefully printed the label, and then gummed it down flat. Next he took a stamped air-letter from his pocket, posting it in the internal mail box of the post-office.

He took his parcel to the counter and placed it on the scale. 'How much will this be to Australia, please?' he enquired.

The girl behind the counter considered the scale reading loftily and then yanked a guide from under the counter. For some time she ran a varnished scarlet fingernail down the items and then said curtly:

'Two shillings. Registered?'

'Of course. That's why I sealed the knots.'

'That will be two and six.'

Barridge paid the money and took his receipt. Leaving the post office he quickened his steps in the direction of his office.

★　★　★

Gordon Tinsley, estate agent, was one of those terrors of suburbia variously known as 'Nosy Parker,' and 'Smart Aleck'. Hence it was with annoyance that Mr. Brady, on his way to his daily stockbroking, observed Tinsley lumbering up the steps of the No. 11 'bus.

A morning newspaper in which he pretended to be absorbed did not save Mr. Brady from the exuberant greeting. 'Well, well, if it isn't Jim Brady — but with no diamonds to match, eh? Where've you been keeping yourself — ?'

Tinsley plumped down next to Brady, pushing the unfortunate stockbroker hard against the window. Tinsley had a habit of keeping his knees very wide apart. Jim Brady gave a faint smile, glanced at the big, red, grinning face, and then glanced away again.

'You saw me two days ago,' Brady reminded him. 'That isn't such a long time — '

'Even two seconds can be a long time, my lad! Might make all the difference between life and death. Dammit, don't be so retiring! Let the people know what you think, and if they don't like it kick their teeth out. Stand up for your rights!'

Brady glanced round the crowded seats of the upper deck as though looking for a way of escape — and failed to see one.

'Anything worth investing in?' Tinsley asked presently. 'I've money ready — providing it's a dead cert.'

'You'll not find a dead cert in stockbroking any more than you will in horse-racing,' Brady answered. 'Market's very fluid just at present.'

'Too bad,' Tinsley said, pouting. 'When you've a couple of thou to throw about you like to put it somewhere safe.'

'Might try a bank,' Brady said, without enthusiasm. He was reasonably sure that Tinsley did not even have a 'couple of thou. to throw about'. Tinsley was the kind of man who outwardly appeared to bulge with prosperity and money and yet whose home completely belied the fact. He had only one thing in plenty — gift of the gab. Somehow Tinsley kept the ball rolling, supplementing his erratic income with flutters on the horses, dogs, and football matches.

'I'm thinking of getting out of this confounded town,' he said presently, proffering a twenty packet of cigarettes. 'Too limited for a man of my talents. A main street, a few offices, a council that just sits and argues. No use at all. I'd shift 'em quick enough if I were on the council.'

Brady considered as he lighted the cigarette, 'I've always thought of Hadlam as not such a bad little place. There *are* some things which tend to give it a bad name — those cheap shops just off the main street for one thing; that amusement arcade full of stalls and catchpenny gadgets for another. Funny the police don't do something about those.'

'The police!' Tinsley scoffed. 'What do you expect of one superintendent and a detective-sergeant? Let me tell you something, Brady. There's a lot of illegal betting goes on in this town — not with the chap *I* deal with, mind you. Bob King's dead straight. It beats me why the police haven't roped the dodgy ones in. As for the Chief Constable of the county he's probably too preoccupied with his next golf match.'

'That's unfair,' Brady answered. 'The Chief Constable, Colonel Wilton, has done a good deal to promote more sensible regulation around here . . . Don't know about the young superintendent and detective-sergeant. And as for those catchpenny gadgets, maybe the police can't act. I only *think* they're catchpenny. Perhaps, legally they're not.'

'Just the same, Hadlam's still no place

for a go-ahead like me,' Tinsley grinned. 'I was only saying to the little lady this morning — Say,' Tinsley broke off, looking about him. 'What's happened to Bill Barridge this morning? Never known him to miss as long as I've been taking the eleven. Incidentally, he's a bit of a dark horse.'

'Is he?' Brady said boredly, and wiped steam from the window with his newspaper.

Tinsley looked really happy now he had something to work on. 'To look at him you'd say he suffered from a persistent belly-ache, wouldn't you? But it's a pose. All that shy, retiring stuff is a lot of bunk!'

Even Brady's interest was stirred. 'I've always thought that he was one of the mildest men I've ever met.'

'Only on the surface,' Tinsley replied darkly. 'It's my opinion that he's leading a double life.'

'Get out!' Brady scoffed. 'He's got a fifteen-stone wife and three kids. He wouldn't dare step out of line for a single moment.'

'I know differently,' Tinsley grinned. 'I met him in town the other day with a young woman, and a very nice piece of blonde homework she was, too. He introduced her to me — made no effort to keep it a secret. Said her name was Mrs. Carr, so if she's not a widow she must be a hot number too, eh? I might have thought it was only a business arrangement the first time, but I also saw them in town on another occasion, in the evening after office hours.' Tinsley paused and winked solemnly.

'Take it from me, my lad, that means something! Not that I blame him, mind. Must get pretty dull for him in that solicitor's office and a wife like he's got . . . I can do with a bit of a frisk myself, sometimes.'

'Talk of the devil,' Brady murmured, looking through the window, 'there *is* Barridge now!'

'Eh?' Tinsley leaned over and stared through the roughly cleared circle on the window. Below, just emerging from the amusement arcade with an umbrella on this arm, Barridge was walking sedately, a circular brown paper parcel in his right hand.

'It's him all right,' Tinsley agreed. 'Wonder what he's got in that parcel of his? I'll lay evens it isn't something for his missus. For that blonde piece, I bet you! Looks as though he shaved in the dark,' Tinsley added, grinning. 'Look at the size of that chunk of cotton-wool on his jaw!'

Then the 'bus had swung aside into the traffic and the figure of William Barridge was hidden from view . . .

The legal firm of Henry Minton, solicitor and Commissioner-for-Oaths, was situated in somewhat dingy offices. They occupied three rooms on the first floor of a converted Georgian dwelling-house and to reach them one had to enter by the yellow portico with its faded pillars, pass along a length of dusty hall, and then mount a flight of uncarpeted stairs, illumined by a grimy skylight.

The bottom floor was occupied by the caretaker-janitor and his wife, their living quarters being at the left-hand back of the stairs where a glass inset in the door gave them a view of all the people who entered or left the building. It was his duty to give undesirables short shrift — but so far such prowess had not been called for. The only people who came and went in and out of Chertsey House were either the staffs or clients of Minton's, Barraclough's, the insurance agents, on the second floor, or the architects on the top floor.

Into the greyness of the hall at 9.20 hurried William Barridge, five minutes behind his usual time. Baxter, the janitor, was in the act of mopping the linoleum which led to his own quarters and was glad of the excuse to pause and greet the familiar head clerk of Minton's.

''Morning, Mr. Barridge. Cold again.'

'Very cold, Baxter,' Barridge agreed. 'And this building wouldn't grow tomatoes very fast either!'

'No, sir,' the janitor grinned. 'I'm doing my best with the steam heater. Precious little fuel we get these days.'

Barridge mounted the stairs, turning in at the main door on the first landing inscribed *Henry Minton — Enquiry — Walk In.* From behind the frosted glass panel came the sound of voices, which continued as Barridge entered the main office.

'Good *morning*, Mr. Barridge!' greeted Sally Higson, the typist, and made a tremendous pretence of dusting her typewriter.

''Morning,' said Standish, the tall, lank-haired junior clerk, who took himself very seriously.

''Mornin',' added Jimmy, the office boy, and dropped a mystery magazine deftly into the waste bin.

'Good morning,' Barridge replied dis-interestedly. Dragging his bunch of keys out of his pocket he selected the Yale for his own office door, jabbed it in the lock and let himself in . . . There were three doors to the offices — Barridge's, Henry Minton's, and the main door. Each lock was a Yale, though underneath them were preposterous keyholes dating from the time when a dungeon-like key had been used, until Minton had decided to become a little more streamlined. Now these old locks and keyholes were redundant — unless to peep through. But so far there had never been anything worth peeping at.

Barridge went over to the gas-fire and

lighted it, pulled his packet of sandwiches out of his pocket and laid it on the desk; then he got out of his hat and coat and rubbed his hands.

The office smelled of ink, dry parchment, cold air, and Monday morning. The window had frosted itself completely, mercifully obscuring the view of uninspiring yards and the backs of houses.

Barridge went over to his desk and sat down. He tore Saturday and Sunday from the calendar and mused over the text for Monday. 'The best way to get rid of your duties is to discharge them.' A faint smile flickered across his face. He dropped his gaze to the memo sheet below the quotation and observed that he had written:

Mr. Minton. Appointment in Liverpool

'Yes . . . ' Barridge reflected, then tore off the memo, burned it deliberately in the ashtray and tossed the charred remains into the waste bin. 'Liverpool. That's what he said.'

He pressed a bell-push. In the outer

office Jimmy dropped his thriller magazine into his pocket, and shambled across to Barridge's door. He knocked and entered, stood waiting, a calflick of brown hair down his forehead.

'Mr. Minton come yet?' Barridge asked him briefly.

'No, sir — an' I never heard of him coming before ten neither. Why should he? He's the boss.'

'Less sauce from you, Jimmy. Outside — and let me know when he arrives.'

The office boy glanced at the parcel at the end of the desk, then went out again and shut the door. He paused, considering Sally Higson's by no means shapeless leg as she adjusted the seam in her stocking.

'That show?' she asked the junior clerk. 'It's darned.'

'Nobody'll notice the darn,' Standish grinned. 'Not the men, anyway.'

'Unless I'm careful,' Sally continued, Standish's implication sailing right over her head, 'there'll be a ladder soon. And this is the only pair I can spare without using my best. Can't use those: I've got a date tonight.'

She put her foot back on the floor from the chair edge, twisted her head like a parrot to survey herself backwards, then plumped in the seat before the typewriter.

She slammed the carriage to maximum left. 'I'm cut out for better things, I am. Not that I mind typing so much — but all these 'whereases' and 'Aforesaids' make me dizzy. And as for abstracts of title — ! I think old Baggage gives them to me on purpose to fill in the time.'

'*Mr.* Barridge to you,' the office boy corrected. 'And take care how you treat him today, Sally. He's a bit sharp.'

'Him! Sharp!' Sally's blue eyes were scornful.

'He is a bit spineless at that,' Standish admitted. 'Gets on my nerves, the way he wheedles to the boss. Now, if I were in Baggage's place — *Good* morning, Mr. Minton,' Standish broke off, with a fixed smile as the ruler of the firm suddenly entered.

'Good morning, Standish — Miss Higson — Jimmy. Mr. Barridge here?'

'Yes, sir,' Jimmy answered. 'He's in his

office. He asked me to tell him when you had arrived.'

'Send him in,' Minton ordered, and pulled out the Yale from the bunch that opened his office door. He swept within and slammed the door with that lack of courtesy peculiar to some employers.

3

'You're just as bad as Baggage,' Sally Higson murmured sweetly, looking at Standish. 'Scared stiff of the old boy!'

'I said *if* I were in Baggage's place,' Standish replied, with inspiration.

Sally sniffed, batted out 'Abstract of Title of all that messuage or dwelling-house ... ' and took no more notice, only raising her eyes from the keyboard as Barridge came out of his office, tugged at his tie, felt at the lump of cotton-wool on his jaw, and then gave a genteel knock on the ruler's door.

'Come in!' Minton snapped, and added, 'Good morning!' like a couple of gunshots as he frowned at his correspondence.

'Good morning, sir,' Barridge's voice was as servile as ever. 'Very cold again.'

'What the devil else do you expect in February?'

Barridge remained silent. He knew

exactly why he had been sent for — to take the bunch of keys lying on the desk and open the strong room where all the firm's deeds were kept. So he waited for permission — and gazed.

Henry Minton was stout, very broad across the shoulders with a florid face and wealth of black hair. In a clumsy kind of way he was even good-looking, except for the bulbous end of his nose that spoiled the effect. A little too much imbibing was the main cause of this tendency to polypus, just as it was revealed in the slight shakiness of his thick hands and the raspy breathing that came from him as he read the letters.

'Well?' he snapped, glancing up. 'What the devil are you waiting for, Barridge? Take those keys and get the strong room opened. You may need something from there while I'm away today.'

'Yes, sir . . . Liverpool, you said?'

Henry Minton sliced through the top of an envelope with the eight-inch blade of the antique knife he used as a letter-opener. 'That's right — Liverpool. Any objections?'

'No, sir. I just wanted to verify the fact since I shall be in charge — .'

'Dammit, man, you've known for a fortnight that I'm going to Liverpool today — on the ten-thirty. Important business. If anything turns up you'll know how to handle it. Now go and get that strong room opened. Bring the keys back.'

'Of course, sir.' Barridge took the keys and departed.

'Damned weak-kneed fool,' Minton muttered, and tossed down the knife on his desk. 'No more spirit than present-day whisky.'

He finished reading his correspondence and then looked around in an effort to call to mind anything he ought to take away with him. It was a big office with one high, frost-coated window that gave on to a yard. The catch was an extremely stiff one, and at the top of the window was a rather faded pair of curtains. To reach them demanded the use of a long, thin, rough-wood lath that now stood in a corner, awaiting use when the summer — if any — poured burning sunshine

31

through the glass.

There was a big and extremely heavy desk with one chair, in which Minton now sat, before it. The chair was an antique he had picked up cheap at a sale, its high wooden back worked into all manner of scrolls, loops, slits and circles . . . Filing cabinets, two hide armchairs for visitors, an Axminster carpet showing signs of wear, completed the appointments, except for the inevitable private safe supported on glazed bricks in a corner, and the telephone on the desk.

Barridge returned with his gentle knock and handed the keys back. 'Thank you, sir. I've opened the strong room door.'

'Right . . . ' Minton scooped the keys back into his pocket and got to his feet, walked across to the tall polished oak stand by the door where his hat and coat were hanging. 'Didn't you want to see me about something? Jimmy said so.'

'Oh, I was merely going to remind you that you intended going to Liverpool, sir. In case you had forgotten.'

'Well I hadn't. And since it's confidential business on which I'm going,

Barridge, no word to anybody. Understand?'

'You mean that if anybody should enquire as to where you are I am not to tell them?'

'Exactly. If anything comes in you can handle it well enough. I'm not sure when I'll be back, so in case of anything important leave a note on my blotter . . . Oh, how's that mortgage for Johnstone going on?'

'I have it in hand, sir, and Standish is finishing off the details.'

'See that it's finished for tomorrow. Johnstone will be coming in. He's too valuable a client for us to play around.'

'I quite agree.'

'You would,' Minton observed sourly. He heaved into his overcoat, adjusted his black homburg, then left the office with Barridge behind him. The lock on Minton's door snapped shut. With scarcely a glance at his staff the ruler swept out and slammed the main door behind him.

'Is Boozy likely to be away long?' Standish asked.

'One of these days, Standish, Mr.

Minton is going to come in and hear you call him that,' Mr. Barridge warned him.

Standish grinned. 'I'll bet it costs him a fortune in whisky these days. Anyway, how long is he going to be?'

'I haven't the slightest idea.' And as he saw the brightening faces of the junior clerk, typist, and office boy, Barridge added mildly: 'And don't interpret that as an excuse for slackness. There's a lot to be done. You're doing those abstracts, Miss Higson?'

'Yes, Mr. Barridge,' she sighed. 'In triplicate.'

'That's right. And you, Standish, are fixing up the legal details on that Johnstone mortgage? Mr. Minton will want to attend to it tomorrow.'

'I'm doing it,' the junior clerk acknowledged.

Barridge nodded. 'Good. If anybody comes I'll be in my office.'

He walked across to it and closed the door behind him. Sally stopped typing. 'Y'know,' she said reflectively, 'there's something *wrong* with this office, and I used to think it was old Boozy who caused it with his periodic tantrums. But now I think life would be much pleasanter here without Baggage. Boozy isn't much trouble because he's out such a lot, but Baggage . . . '

'What do you think we ought to do?' asked the office boy, who was supposed to be adding up the stamp account. 'Bump him off? I know lots of ways . . . Look here!'

Surreptitiously he brought to view from his jacket the thriller magazine that had been absorbing him at intervals. It was one of the more lurid types of American pulps. The glaring letters on the cover conveyed the fact that it was a confessional story with the spine-crawling title — *I Killed My Boss!*

''Sgood!' Jimmy enthused, his eyes bright. 'You'd never think of killing anybody the way this dame did.'

'Dame?' Sally looked vague. 'You mean a *girl* killed her boss?'

'Sure did. He got fresh with her.'

'But Boozy never got fresh with me,' Sally pointed out. 'And old Baggage just couldn't. In fact,' she added rather miserably, 'nobody *ever* got fresh with me — not even when I felt sure they would. I'm no film star, of course, but I'm sure I'm worth being made a pass at . . . '

The clicking of the machine resumed and Jimmy forgot all about the stamp account as he lost himself in the gory details of the novelette. Then a well-aimed paper fastener stung him sharply on the ear.

'Get your work done,' growled Standish. 'What do you suppose you're paid for?'

Having got the general office on to something resembling an even keel Standish ploughed through the wearying details of the Johnstone mortgage. The typewriter clicked steadily, pausing only now and again as Sally made references to her latest boy friends or the newest films she had seen.

To relieve the monotony at eleven o'clock Sally downed tools and went along the landing to fill the kettle from the tap in the poky little mousetrap which served as a bathroom-lavatory. She flushed the kettle out with water three times only because it took longer than doing it once. On the top of this, before she even commenced operations, she always allowed the water to run for several minutes to prevent what she called 'taste of the pipe'.

When she eventually returned to the general office she knocked on Mr. Barridge's door and entered.

'It's eleven o'clock, Mr. Barridge. Here's some water for your tea. Shall I put it on for you?'

'If you will,' William Barridge assented, pondering something.

Sally's eyes strayed momentarily to the packet on the desk — Mr. Barridge's inevitable lunch, she realized — then she went across to the ring on top of the gas-fire and turned away wincing as she held a match to it.

With an explosive pop it ignited and she poured half the water from the kettle into the aluminium pan Mr. Barridge used exclusively for himself. She took as long as possible over the job, which included taking teapot, tin of tea, condensed milk, saccharin and cup and saucer from the corner cupboard. The longer she took the nearer it brought her to lunchtime.

'All fixed, Mr. Barridge,' she said finally.

'Thanks, Miss Higson.' Barridge did not look up. He went on reading correspondence and fingering the chunk of cotton wool on his jaw.

Returning to her own domain Sally spent another ten minutes making and drinking tea with Standish and the office boy, huddled round the gas-fire beneath the old-fashioned imitation marble mantelshelf.

'I have the idea,' Sally said finally, 'that old Baggage has got something on his mind. Something,' she finished wisely, 'is bothering him.'

'Nuts to him,' Jimmy said tersely.

Sally sighed and shook her blonde head. 'This is no life for a girl,' she complained. 'No wonder that dame in your story bumped off the boss. What did she do? Cut his throat?'

'You really want to know?' Jimmy asked eagerly. 'It tells you all about it on page nine. The heroine is very beautiful — a real smasher with hair like flowing honey and lips the color of rubies — or was it cherries? Then there's a man in the office who has black wavy hair, all glossy like a boot polish advertisement, and the sort of lips the girl wants to kiss . . . '

'Oh, shut up!' Standish snorted, and mooched back to his own desk to continue working. He felt he had an example to maintain, and he was not ungallant enough to add that a beautiful girl might have improved matters immensely. Sally Higson was simply not beautiful; that was the trouble.

Standish's example of industry had perforce to be followed by the others. A further ten minutes was used up in putting away the pots and kettle, then Sally settled herself for the last hectic hour and twenty minutes until lunch at one.

Barridge emerged from his office now and again and to go across to the strong room. Once, as she watched him enter this baby vault, Sally had a tremendous impulse to dash forward and shut the heavy steel door upon him — but instead she went on typing.

The strong room was a fad on Minton's part. Actually it was an inlet in the wall, which had once been a microscopic box room. Now it was lined with steel shelves upon which reposed all the deeds of the firm, whilst the floor was taken up with tin boxes having such cheerful inscriptions as 'Jones Deceased', 'Billings Deceased', 'Safe Custody of Mather's Exors' and so on.

Having obtained what he wanted, Barridge returned to his office and closed the door. Sally said 'Blast!' as she felt a ladder run up the whole length of her darned stocking. Getting up from her chair she retired to the mousetrap and hunted round for the soap, the makeshift to which she usually flew when a disaster of this kind occurred.

She came back into the office looking annoyed.

'Hasn't anybody brought any soap yet?' she demanded. 'Anyway, who took it in the first place? Was it you, Jimmy?'

'No — I never saw the soap, and I didn't take it last Thursday when you said it went. Why, you don't need a wash, do you?'

'Why can't people leave things alone?' Sally moaned. 'Soap's been gone since last Thursday and I keep forgetting to bring any.'

With a further anguished glance at her ruined stocking she returned to continue with her work.

Time lumbered on to 12.55, at which time the five minutes preparation for departure commenced. Sally was still saying she just couldn't walk down the street with her stockings in such a state and wondered whether to dispense with both of them entirely — to which idea Standish inclined favorably — when Barridge came out of his office, contemplating his watch.

'Off to lunch, eh?' he asked briefly.

'In a moment, sir, yes,' Standish agreed. 'Nothing important before lunch, is there?'

'No. But be prompt in returning, though. I've a lot of fresh abstracts for you, Miss Higson.'

'Yes, Mr. Barridge.' She smiled woodenly.

It struck Standish, the brightest of the trio, that it was odd for Barridge to ask if they were going to lunch. Usually he never bothered himself in the least where they were going. Unless it was that with Minton being away he considered it was his duty to keep an eye on the proceedings.

'You'll be staying for lunch, Mr. Barridge?' Standish asked. 'As usual?'

'Yes. I have my sandwiches. Don't like a heavy meal in the middle of the day. Bad for the digestion.'

'Yes, sir,' Standish agreed, wondering if it really was: then as the office clock pointed exactly to one he opened the outer door and followed Sally and Jimmy out on to the landing.

Barridge closed the door behind them and stood pondering; then he walked back slowly into his office.

★ ★ ★

Fortified by Irish stew and a liberal plateful of cabinet pudding and thick custard, Sally Higson puffed her way up the stairs. She was still breathing laboriously as she took hold of the office doorknob to twist it. To her surprise she found the door solid and unyielding. For the first time in her experience as typist to Minton the outer door was locked at lunchtime.

She was not desperately anxious to get back to her typewriter. Standish would be here shortly with his key, and that would be soon enough. So she propped herself against the wall, dug a caramel from the bag of them she had in her pocket, and chewed reflectively.

There presently came a clattering of feet and they accompanied Jimmy, a cap low down over his eyes, scarf knotted gigantically at his throat, and immense cycling gauntlets on his hands.

'What's cooking, kid?' he asked, lapsing into his usual cinematic vernacular. 'How's the stocking? Get it fixed?'

'Mind your own business,' Sally retorted. 'If you must know I'm wearing my best pair — all because you pinched the soap.'

'I didn't!'

'Well, anyway,' Sally said, 'I've brought a piece with me for washing our hands.'

43

'Say, what's up?' Jimmy went on. 'What are you stuck out here for?'

'Door's locked.' Sally chewed lambently. 'Old Baggage must have gone out, or something.'

'More likely he's gone to sleep. Whoever heard of Baggage going out at lunchtime?' Bracing his back against the wall Jimmy slid down into a squatting position and pulled out his magazine. From that moment his conversation, never on a high intellectual plane anyway, evaporated completely as he went further into the details of how Miss Maisie Ballanski had blotted out her too amorous boss.

Then came Standish, in his neat overcoat and soft hat, looking curiously self-conscious. He gave a start. 'What's this?' he asked blankly.

'Place locked up,' Jimmy said, struggling up and putting his magazine away. 'Can stay that way for all I care. Only I suppose you've got a key?'

'Of course I have . . . ' Standish reached in his trouser pocket. Feeling just like the boss he jammed the key in the lock and turned it. They all entered. For some reason they were a trifle wide-eyed, expecting to see something totally unexpected in the general office, but it was just the same — stuffy, smelling of gas-fire fumes, with their littered desks just as they had left them.

'Aw, heck,' Jimmy grumbled, putting all their thoughts into words. 'I'd sort of expected something thrilling to explain the locked door.'

'What did you expect?' Standish asked, grinning. 'A body dripping with gore and half a dozen daggers stuck in it?'

'Please!' Sally complained, making a face. 'I've only just had a big lunch — '

They took off their hats and coats. Sally held a lighted match at arm's length and set her teeth as she ignited the gas fire. Jimmy grinned at her terrified expression; then Standish, who had been looking thoughtful, went over to the door of Barridge's office and knocked lightly.

There was no response. He tried the door gently and found it locked. 'He must have been called away on urgent business,' he shrugged. 'Naturally he'd have to close the place up.'

'Then why is that open?' Sally asked, nodding to the wide open door of the strong room. 'He couldn't lock it without Boozy's keys, of course, but he could have shut it.'

Standish went across to his desk and rustled his hands through the mortgage of Johnstone. Sally warmed her knees and hands for about ten minutes and then went to her typewriter. As she sat down she beamed.

'Baggage can stay away as long as he likes,' she declared blissfully. 'I've no abstracts to do. Finished 'em this morning. In which case . . . ' She stooped to the stationery drawer of her desk and from it took a novel. With another caramel to help her, she soon lost all consciousness of the office and its humdrum activities.

'Makes you think, though,' Jimmy said presently, and Standish glanced at him. 'I wonder if Baggage got fed up with being picked on by the boss and cleared out? We all know he leads a dog's life with the boss — and from the various hints that get dropped he doesn't do much better at home either. Wouldn't surprise me if he's just hopped it.'

Restless at having nothing in particular to do, and also possessing an abnormally inquisitive mind, Jimmy began to prowl about the office. Standish took no more notice. He had his hands full with whereases and aforesaids. And Sally was lost to the world.

Therefore Jimmy's sudden mighty yell had something of the effect of a falling bomb. He was just rising from before the locked door of Henry Minton's office where apparently he had been peering through the ancient keyhole. '*Bloody hell*!' he whispered.

Standish got irritably to his feet. 'What's wrong with you?' he snapped — and Sally, her peace shattered, shifted her feet aimlessly.

'I — I don't quite know,' Jimmy gasped, his face pale. 'Look for yourself.'

Standish went over to the keyhole of Minton's door. The view beyond was circumscribed, but it was enough. The scene was clad in grey afternoon light.

The heavy high-backed chair that Minton invariably used was overturned, and there seemed to be a suggestion of confusion about the top of the desk.

But these factors receded before the vision of a body lying on the floor, face down, from the back of which the hilt of a large knife was projecting.

4

Standish took a hold of himself and got to his feet again. He held out a hand to stop Sally as she tried to follow him in looking through the keyhole.

'What is it?' she demanded, piqued.

'It's a man!' Jimmy blurted out. 'Dead! A knife's sticking out of his back.'

'Lor'! But — but who is it? Boozy?'

Standish bent to the keyhole again. He was at it for several seconds; then he straightened up and shook his head. 'No, it isn't Boozy . . . It's Barridge.'

'Barridge!' Sally gasped. 'In there? Dead?'

'Bloody hell!' Jimmy muttered again, staring at the closed door. 'How'd he get in there, anyway? The boss is the only one with a key to the door.'

Standish had a sudden realization of tragedy. He gave up trying to stop Sally looking, and instead dived for the telephone. He swung the dial-face to its limit.

'Number please?'

'The police — quick!' Standish snapped.

With commendable rapidity he was connected to a deep-voiced sergeant-in-charge. 'Hadlam Constabulary. Hello?'

'Oh — This is Minton's — that is, Henry Minton, solicitor, twelve Parkhurst Street. You'd better come over. Somebody's dead — murdered . . . '

'Murdered!' the sergeant exclaimed.

'Looks like it. Our head clerk is lying with a knife in his back. I can just see him through the keyhole.'

'Keyhole? Are you sure you haven't made a mistake, sir?'

'Of course I haven't!' Standish retorted. 'It looks as though there's been some kind of a struggle as well.'

'It does, eh? All right, give me the details. Who's that speaking?'

Standish told everything, in fits and starts, and the sergeant finished with the assurance that Superintendent Henshaw would be over immediately with a divisional-surgeon. Nothing was to be touched, nobody was to leave, and the room where the body lay was not to be disturbed.

'As if it could be,' Sally Higson commented nervously. 'Door's locked and only Boozy has the key. Come to think of it, that's a bit strange . . . isn't it?' Her voice trailed off.

Standish sat down perplexedly. 'We'll be questioned. You realize that?'

'I'm not worried,' Sally replied. 'I went home to lunch as usual — and I can prove it.'

'I went to the Crescent Café, but I don't know whether *I* can prove it.' Standish said slowly. 'The place was pretty crowded and I don't often go there: my usual place was full up. Don't suppose anybody would remember me.'

Jimmy had an inspiration. 'Why don't we ask old Baxter? He sees most of what goes on. That's what detectives do in the stories I've read, and they wouldn't be printed if it wasn't correct. I think we should tell the police that they should grill Baxter and give him the old one-two.'

Standish shook his head. 'We'd better not tackle Baxter. It's a job for the police, not us. Less we try and do, the better . . . You know,' Standish grinned awkwardly, 'this could develop into a pretty unpleasant mess. Now, I wonder . . . ?'

He went across to Barridge's office and stooped to the keyhole, peering through. All he could see was the edge of a desk and the outlines of a brown paper parcel tied with string.

'Nothing there,' he announced, straightening — and Sally looked, and then Jimmy, who gave a little gasp.

'Nothing there? But there is. There's his lunch, on the end of the desk. I saw it there when I went in to see him this morning.'

'So did I when I took in the water for his tea.' Sally looked surprised. 'But why didn't he eat it?'

'Look here!' Standish spoke with unexpected authority. 'No use conjecturing. We've simply got to wait until the police come . . . Pity we don't know where to contact the boss. Might 'phone his wife, perhaps?' He shook his head. 'No. See what the police have to say.'

Standish and Sally drifted back to their respective desks and sat in silence. Jimmy settled himself on one of the three chairs usually provided for visitors, and scowled deeply. He was thinking that he had read enough thrillers to be able to investigate the mystery for himself. A meek and mild clerk being suddenly discovered dead in a locked office with a knife in his back was something that definitely required investigation . . .

Then at last there were voices in the corridor and a sudden sharp rap on the door. It opened even as Standish got to his feet and a man in police superintendent's uniform came in. Behind him was a sergeant and two constables.

'I'm Superintendent Henshaw,' explained the man in the peaked uniform-cap. 'This is Detective-sergeant Willis . . . I take it you are Mr. Standish, who rang us up?'

'Yes, sir,' Standish acknowledged. 'He — that is our head clerk — is in there. We've seen him through the keyhole.'

The superintendent went over to the locked door of Minton's office and peered through the hole intently; then he straightened. 'Who has the key to this door?' he asked.

'Only Mr. Minton,' Standish replied. 'The door hasn't been opened since he left. He didn't say where he was going, but he's been absent since about quarter-past ten this morning.'

'But surely there's some way to contact him? What instructions were left in case anything important turned up?'

'He may have told Mr. Barridge something, but he certainly didn't tell any of us.'

'The room has a window, I suppose?' the Superintendent asked.

'Yes. Overlooking the yard at the back.'

'Then we'll get into the office that way. This door is too massive to break down, and I don't want to disturb the lock either until it's been examined. Barton!'

One of the constables came forward. 'Sir?'

'Ring up Glover, the locksmith, and ask him if he can come over right away. You, boy . . . ' The superintendent turned to the awe-stricken Jimmy. 'What's your name?'

'Jimmy Elgate, sir.'

'All right. Jimmy.' A faint smile crossed the superintendent's square, still young face. 'You'll show us where the yard is. And you,' Henshaw added, to the remaining policeman, 'stay on watch on the landing. I'll have a word with you, Mr. Standish, later — and with the young lady. Come with me, Willis.'

Proud at having been selected as a guide, Jimmy led the way down the stairs to the outdoors. He glanced at the police car parked at the kerb, walked a few yards along the street, and then stopped at a high wooden gate — a door in fact — set in the center of a brick wall which rose quite eight feet.

'There's a cul-de-sac beyond this door, sir,' Jimmy explained, as the superintendent waited, the detective-sergeant beside him. 'Only people who use it are the janitor, or the chaps who bring the coal and clean the windows. Usually the janitor gets into this yard by going through the basement under his own quarters and opening up the coal trapdoor. On the other hand I can shin over the wall and open the gate for you.'

'Right — do that,' and the superintendent gave the boy a hand.

Reaching the top, Jimmy dropped on the other side, then drew back the bolts. Henshaw and Willis walked into an area about twelve feet long by eight square. One side of it was made up by Chertsey House itself. The windows of the ground floor were at the back of the building, so the first window visible from this viewpoint, one floor up, was that of Minton's office.

Above it was a corresponding window belonging to the insurance agents, and above again the window of the architects . . . Henshaw craned back his neck to look at them and then studied the view that faced the windows. It was the blank wall of the next building, reaching to approximately the same total height as Chertsey House. At the opposite end of the yard was another eight foot high wall, but without a door.

'Looks as if we'll need a ladder, sir,' Willis remarked.

'The janitor's got one,' Jimmy volunteered. 'Shall I go and tell him?'

'Stay here, son,' the superintendent instructed — and jerked his head to Willis who left the yard quickly.

Thus subdued Jimmy said no more and stood waiting as the superintendent glanced about him again and finally at the ground. It was concreted, dipping from the sides towards the center to carry off rainwater into a single drain set in the centre of the yard. Near the gateway was the wooden trapdoor Jimmy had mentioned.

The superintendent went over to it.

'That's the only back way out there is for Baxter,' Jimmy explained. 'Bit old-fashioned — it should have been pulled down long ago, if you ask me.'

Willis reappeared, bearing an extension ladder over his shoulder. He set it up against the side of the house, opened the extension, and then began to climb, the superintendent keeping his foot pressed hard against the bottom rung. The detective-sergeant busied himself at the window and then glanced below.

'No chance of opening this from the outside, sir,' he said. 'The catch is across and it's a pretty rusty one.'

'Then break the window,' Henshaw ordered.

Willis nodded and drove his elbow at the lower left side of the window, smashing a small hole. Reaching inside he struggled hard with the catch, forced it back, then raised the big square sash. The superintendent turned to Jimmy.

'Keep your foot on this ladder, son, while I go up. Afterwards tell the janitor to move it, and you go back to the office.'

'Yes, sir,' Jimmy assented, and the superintendent began the climb to the window, heaved himself over the sill and into the office beyond. He surveyed the scene, Willis beside him.

The man on the floor, whom Standish had said was Barridge, was laying face down, parallel with the desk, the hilt of a knife projecting from a spot just below his left shoulder blade. The hilt of the knife was dull gunmetal grey and had a crosspiece of unusual length, quite three inches. Barridge's hands were flung out in front of him and one leg was slightly drawn up beneath his body.

His face, somewhat on one side, had a chunk of cotton wool adhering to the jaw. His dark coat, whcre the knife had entered, was rendered much darker in an uneven circle where blood had flowed. Beside him — nearly on top of him — was the heavy antique chair that Minton always used. The desk was in disorder: two heavy legal books were on the floor and the rug in front of the extinguished gas-fire was rumpled. Over by the door one of the hide armchairs had been shifted out of position and lay with one side pressed hard against the wall.

'Looks as if there's been some fun in here, sir,' Willis commented.

The superintendent nodded, his gaze encompassing the filing cabinets, the private safe, the tall lath standing in a corner, the bookcase full of works on regulations and legal schedules. Then he looked down at the body.

'Can't do anything until our divisional-surgeon, Paget, gets here,' he said. 'He said when I 'phoned him that he'd come right away, so he shouldn't be long. Same goes for the fingerprint and photograph boys.'

Henshaw walked to the door. First he inspected the old-fashioned lock set low down, a considerable distance below the Yale lock. Squatting he peered through it and it gave him a view into the office beyond.

'Standish could have seen in here, just as he said,' he commented, getting up. 'Now what about this?'

He inspected the milled edge of the Yale lock knob. Taking it in his handkerchief he turned it and opened the office door, stepped outside and contemplated Standish, Sally, and Jimmy as they sat waiting for him, wide-eyed. At the superintendent's nod P.C. Barton went into Minton's office and almost closed the door.

'While I'm waiting for the doctor and experts to arrive I'll see what you three can tell me,' Henshaw decided. 'I'll take each of you separately . . . ' He glanced at the adjoining door of Barridge's office. 'What about that? Can you get in?'

'Locked,' Standish answered. 'The keys will be on Mr. Barridge. That is — er — the body.'

'That being so, you, Jimmy, and you Miss — er — had better wait in the corridor outside for a moment. I want each of your statements in private. You remain here, Mr. Standish.'

Sally and the office boy went out, the constable on the landing closing the door after them.

'Now, Mr. Standish . . . ' The superintendent settled himself at Sally's desk and took off his uniform-cap. He was a dark-haired, hook-nosed man of perhaps thirty-eight, with a purposeful jaw and keen grey eyes.

Henshaw pulled a small notebook out of his pocket and put it on the desk. Then he tugged out a pencil and held it in his right hand. At Standish's own desk the detective-sergeant also seated himself and opened a notebook.

'Don't be alarmed, Mr. Standish,' Henshaw smiled. 'Your statement must of course be taken down, typed, and then given to you to read and you will sign it. Nothing to be disturbed about. Can you give me your full name and address, please?'

'Arthur Leonard Standish, fourteen Luke's Court. Hadlam, of course.'

'And what is your position with this firm, Mr. Standish?'

'I'm the junior clerk. I was directly under Mr. Barridge and took my instructions from him. He took them from Mr. Minton, our employer.'

'Then Mr. Barridge was a kind of second employer? In charge of everything?'

'Yes.'

'Do you know how long he had been with this firm?'

'Twenty years. And he often said it was twenty years too long.'

'I understand ... Now follow me, please.'

The superintendent led the way back into the murder office, and motioned. 'The body, Mr. Standish ... Are you sure it is Mr. Barridge?'

Standish went forward, winced, then turned aside. 'Yes — definitely,' he muttered.

'Thank you. Is there anything else you can add which I should know? Anything about this office that is unusual — apart from the signs of upset?'

Standish looked about him, and shook his head. 'Looks the same as ever to me.'

'What about that long lath there in the corner? Is that a usual thing in this office?'

Standish smiled faintly. 'Usual enough, sir. You'll notice that the window is an extra high one. Mr. Minton uses that lath to draw over the curtains — either at night or in the summer time.'

'I see.' Standish's eyes came back to the body. 'There's one thing,' he added. 'About — that knife. Mr. Minton uses it to open his correspondence. I recognize the hilt. It's a souvenir of some kind he got from somewhere.'

'I'll come to that later,' the superintendent said, 'when the doctor and the fingerprint expert have finished. Shall we resume in the outer office?'

Standish followed the superintendent back to Sally's desk, then he glanced up as in a body the divisional-surgeon, a fingerprint expert, and a photographer arrived, each carrying the tools of his calling. The constable in Minton's office motioned within and closed the door. The superintendent began to speak and then stopped as yet another man came in.

'Oh, hello, Glover. Just take that Yale lock apart and let me know if it has been tampered with, will you?'

'Glad to oblige,' the local locksmith assented — an expert whose skill with locks and their intricacies had often helped the police — and with his bag of tools in hand he went into the office.

'What sort of a man was Mr. Barridge, Mr. Standish?' the superintendent asked, sitting back in the chair.

'A retiring sort of chap — always seemed to be being ordered about. He had a great deal to put up with from Mr. Minton.'

'Oh? In what way?'

'Well, the boss is the officious sort — wants everything done on the spur of the moment and is ready to cut your throat if you don't comply. He led old Barridge no end of a dance sometimes. Mr. Minton left most of the arrangements to Barridge, which entailed a lot of responsibility. I often wondered how he stood for the boss's tantrums.'

'Would you say Mr. Barridge and Mr. Minton were enemies?'

'Oh, no, nothing like that. Only Mr. Minton is such a powerful personality and Mr. Barridge was so meek. It was only natural that Mr. Minton would browbeat a weaker man.'

'And how did you feel towards Mr. Barridge?'

'To be frank I thought he was weak. But I got on all right with him personally.'

'I suppose you know Mr. Barridge's address?'

'Yes. Twenty-four Cedar Avenue — just on the outskirts of Hadlam.'

'Thanks.' Henshaw glanced across the room. 'Willis, you might tell Barton to go over to twenty-four Cedar Avenue and break the news to Mrs. Barridge. He'd better take the car and drive her to the mortuary. The body will be there shortly and I want her to formally identify it.'

The detective-sergeant nodded, looked in Minton's office and gave Barton his instructions. Then he settled at the desk again.

'But didn't *I* identify him, sir?' Standish asked, mystified.

'Of course, and I believe you — but a second corroboration from his wife will help. While we are about it, what is Mr. Minton's address?'

'The Elms, Shinley Close. That's the swell quarter of the town, as you probably know.'

'Yes, I know . . . ' Henshaw made a note. 'Well, now let me see. You said that the only person having the key to that private office is Mr. Minton himself — which suggests that Mr. Barridge could only have got in there if Mr. Minton had opened the door for him.'

Standish nodded, startled. If only Minton could have opened the door, then did that not mean that Minton — 'Have you seen the key to that door at any time?' Henshaw broke in.

'I'm pretty sure it's a Yale — like the lock. I've never had reason to handle the key personally, but every morning Mr. Barridge used to open the strong room door. The key to it was on Mr. Minton's bunch and the key to his door among them. That's when I used to see it — save for the odd times when I saw Mr. Minton himself use it to open his door.'

Henshaw made a note, then: 'I suppose you go home to lunch — and the young lady and the office-boy?'

Standish leaned forward and explained every detail, not even suppressing the fact that he doubted if his visit to Crescent Café could be verified. What the superintendent thought about this he did not know for he then changed the subject.

'So it was most unusual to find the outer office door locked, was it?' he asked.

'First time it's ever happened. Even more unusual was the fact that Mr. Barridge's door was shut and locked, too. I can't quite understand that.'

'I take it, then, that Mr. Barridge, through always staying here for lunch, kept the place open?'

'The normal method was to keep it open from nine in the morning when I let Miss Higson and Jimmy in, until five-thirty at night when we close. Mr.

Barridge didn't often leave the office all day, unless for some important business reason. Naturally when we found the outer door shut we assumed that *was* the reason until Jimmy, prowling round, looked through the keyhole of Mr. Minton's office and saw the body.'

'And you have no idea if anybody was supposed to call during the lunch hour?'

'Not as far as I know. There *may* have been, of course, but Mr. Barridge would not have told us. He kept most of his business to himself. Secretive sort of chap. Head clerks in a legal firm get that way in time.'

'Do they?' Henshaw smiled enigmatically. 'All right, Mr. Standish, thank you very much. You can go home now.'

'Home?' Standish exclaimed, astonished.

'That's what I said — until the preliminary details are cleared up. If I need you I can get in touch with you quickly enough. I realize,' Henshaw went on dryly, 'that I shall be unable to stop you talking about this affair, but I would suggest that the less said, the better. All right, Willis, let's have Miss Higson in.'

The girl had hardly seated herself before the divisional-surgeon opened the door of Minton's office and motioned briefly. Henshaw got to his feet and went over to him, stepped into the office and closed the door. There was an air of industry upon the room — the photographer and fingerprint expert plying their trades, and the locksmith busily unscrewing the Yale.

'I've done what I can,' the doctor said. 'As far as I can tell at present that knife was the cause of death. It entered below the left scapula and unless I miss my guess it has penetrated the heart from the back. Tell you better when I've made the postmortem. I'm sure it's a direct heart wound because there isn't a great deal of blood: rarely is from a heart injury. Fortunately the knife has been left in the wound, which will make an estimate of the depth possible. Otherwise I might have been up against it. That's the trouble with knife wounds. When the blade's been withdrawn the wound closes on itself owing to the contraction of the muscles underlying the skin and first cellular tissue . . . '

'But you are reasonably sure,' Henshaw said patiently, 'that that knife caused the wound — and death?'

'At the moment I am. I shan't be properly satisfied until after the p.m.' Dr. Paget was renowned for his almost fussy thoroughness. 'It's more rare than one would think to find a wound so perfect that you can say it fits this or that weapon. There *have* been cases where a wound has been made with something else and a knife inserted afterwards, and of course it often happens that the wound is narrower than the knife employed. That's why I say I'm glad the weapon was left in the body. It will help. I've everything to check yet, including the direction of the blow. I can't tell you anything more from a mere preliminary examination.'

'I understand. How long since death occurred?'

'About an hour — maybe a trifle longer. That is — ' the doctor glanced at his watch — 'somewhere about half-past one. It's quarter to three now. That's as near as I can get.'

'Thanks. I'll leave it to you, then, to advise the mortuary and have them come for the body. Okay if I take the knife out?'

'By all means. Give me a call later and I'll let you have all the details.'

'I will,' Henshaw promised.

The doctor departed and Henshaw went on one knee beside the body. Taking hold of the knife by the extreme ends of the very long hilt crosspiece, pressing his fingertips against the slender points, he drew it free and studied it. It was heavier in the hilt than in the blade and all forged in one piece. The handle was dull grey and smooth, the blade double-edged, measuring — by his spring-rule — exactly eight inches.

'Not far short of being a baby sword,' he commented, handing it over carefully to the fingerprint expert. 'And I'm wondering why the devil the killer left it in the body instead of taking it away and disposing of it. Anyway, see what you can get out of it.'

The fingerprint expert nodded and

took it. This done, Henshaw emptied Barridge's pockets, slipping the entire contents into a large envelope from the desk and then putting them away in his own pocket for future examination. Satisfied for the moment he returned into the general office to tackle Sally Higson.

This young lady, distinctly disturbed by events, was free enough with her information. She had had dinner at home, and her mother and two sisters could prove it. Arriving first at the office she had not noticed anything unusual, beyond the main door of the office being locked. Yes, she had liked Mr. Barridge all right, even though she had considered him a bit stupid. He had seemed a bit sharp tempered that morning, a most unusual thing for him. She had taken in the water for his tea at eleven, but had not observed anything peculiar in any way. Everything had been normal, even to the packet of sandwiches on the desk.

Henshaw, making notes, glanced up enquiringly. 'How do you know they were sandwiches, Miss Higson? They were wrapped up in a parcel, you say.'

'He always brought his lunch with him and he always put the package in the same place on the desk — just at the end near the telephone. Many a time I've emptied his waste bin and found the paper and string with crumbs in the paper. Sandwiches will be in there all right. It's still there, unopened.'

'I see,' Henshaw nodded. 'Did you have any reason to think that he might have somebody calling upon him in the lunch hour?'

'The contrary, I'd say,' Sally responded. 'As I was going to lunch he told me that he'd have some more abstracts of title for me when I returned. I imagined that he'd be working on them during lunchtime. Then — I — I suppose something must have happened.'

'Obviously,' the superintendent agreed, with a searching glance of the girl's chunky face. 'You can't call to mind any odd visitors or queer happenings, I suppose? Not necessarily today, but recently?'

'I — er — No, except — ' Sally gave a fatuous smile as a thought seemed to strike her. 'Well, somebody's stolen the soap out of the little wash-room along the passage.' She coloured slightly. 'I use it as a makeshift when I get ladders in my stockings. I went in to get the soap this morning — but it wasn't there. The soap's been missing since last Thursday. A lovely new block of carbolic, too. I've brought a piece with me from home now. I think Jimmy's pinched it. The janitor wouldn't because he's the one who has to put it there. I'd have mentioned it to him only he would only blame us. He's touchy that way. Funny where it went to . . .'

Henshaw moved his pencil on his notebook. 'Thanks, I think that will be all I'll need from you, Miss Higson. You'd better go home for the time being as Mr. Standish has done, and though I cannot order it I would take it as a favour if you would not discuss the matter with anybody. If I need you again I'll get in touch with you.'

'I'm — I'm to just go home? Leave the office?'

'For the time being I am in charge of

the office,' Henshaw explained. 'That's all, Miss Higson.'

Sally left in a mist of wonder. She gave one profound wink at Jimmy as he lounged on the landing, and then went on her way. Jimmy rubbed his hands in anticipation of the fact that he, too, would be told to go home — then he found himself called into the office to run the gauntlet.

He emerged from it very creditably. Long experience in reading thrillers helped him through the more sticky patches with the superintendent, and being an open honest youth, in spite of the inseparable cockiness of his years, he answered every question frankly enough. He verified Sally's assertion that there must be sandwiches in the parcel on Barridge's desk — that he had been the first to spot the body in Mr. Minton's office — that he did not know when Booz — Mr. *Minton* would be back or where he had gone — and that he had found Sally waiting to get into the office when he had come back from his lunch.

'Right,' Henshaw said finally. 'That's all

I need from you, son.'

'There's just one thing I think I ought to tell it to you, sir . . . It's about Miss Higson,' Jimmy explained. 'She did say that things would be much pleasanter in this office without Mr. Barridge. I'm not saying she meant anything by it, but she did *say* it. And she also asked me about a thriller I'm reading. It's about a girl who killed her boss. Quite interested in getting the details, she was.'

'And did you give them to her?' Henshaw asked gravely.

'Well, no — come to think of it, I didn't. The conversation got on to something else.'

Henshaw scribbled something. 'I'll remember it,' he promised. 'Now get off home and keep your mouth shut. I'm relying on you.'

After the boy had left, Henshaw thought for a moment, and then got to his feet.

'Get those various statements typed afterwards, Willis, and have them signed,' he instructed. 'I think you'd better take a look round this building and have a word with the people on the other floors. As far as I can remember from the plates downstairs there are architects on the top floor and insurance agents on the floor above us. They might have some information — or for that matter might even know something about Barridge that hasn't yet been revealed. Anyway, see what they have to say. Somebody might have seen a stranger knocking about.'

'Yes, sir . . . And what about the janitor? I should think he's a likely number.'

'No doubt of it. I'll tackle him myself later. Carry on for the moment.'

The detective-sergeant nodded, put his notebook away and went out. Minton's office door opened and Glover, the locksmith, emerged.

'I've had the lock to bits and put it back again, superintendent,' he said, snapping shut his little bag of tools. 'You can take it from me that there hasn't been any monkey business with that Yale. It's in perfect order. Nothing but a key could ever have opened it. The same goes for the old-fashioned lock, only more so. And as far as I can tell there's no sign of the door having been forced, either.'

'I see.' Henshaw looked thoughtful. 'Thanks, Glover. It's nice to know even if it is disappointing.'

'Just your hard luck, sir.' Glover smiled, shrugging. 'You chaps earn your money. Give me something easier! Well, see you again.'

He left the office and Henshaw scowled at the door of Minton's room; then he lounged inside it to find the photographer just packing up his camera, and the fingerprint expert at the end of his activities with a Folmer-Graflex. His various dusting powders were packed away in the still open equipment case.

'I've got quite a few shots,' the photographer said, 'and I'll send them over to you later in the day.'

'Thanks.' Henshaw nodded to him as he left, and then turned to the fingerprint man. 'How about it, Steve?'

'No lack of prints,' he answered, 'but none of them tally with our friend on the floor there. The prints on the 'phone, filing cabinets, desk and door are chiefly a twinned loop, nine-ridge type. I imagine they must belong to Minton since this is his office. I've got an impression of Barridge's prints — not very good since he's nearly two hours dead, but good enough. He's got a distinctive plain loop ten-ridge with a scar across the first finger of the left hand.'

'And the knife?'

Stephen Carson grimaced. 'Principally blurs. That knife's been handled hundreds of times. What few prints are clear tally with Minton's twinned loop. I'm going to make another examination of it back at Crayley and see what else I can get. I'm pretty sure that only Minton's prints will come out.'

'All right,' Henshaw agreed. 'As soon as you've finished let me have your report. Thanks for everything.'

Left to himself the superintendent stood looking about the office. Though he would have photographs later on to refresh his memory he preferred a first-hand view as well, and he also went through a careful, methodical sketching of everything and its relationship to the nearest object. By degrees he compiled a list of the articles disturbed and the exact position thereof; then with his notebook back in his pocket he went to the window and examined it.

The glass was only broken where he and Willis had effected an entry. The catch, of the type anchoring across both sashes, was extremely stiff. It took a sheer effort of his fingers to move it back and forth. To close a catch like that from outside, perhaps with the aid of string, would be quite impossible. Which in turn linked up with the self-evident fact that nobody had escaped this way and closed the catch after them.

Opening the window's lower sash Henshaw leaned out and studied the yard below. There was the single drain in the centre of the concrete. To the left was the eight-foot wall with the wooden door in it; to the right the eight-foot wall with no door. In front, the blank wall of the opposite building. Above, the windows of the insurance agents and architects respectively.

Then, for a moment, the wintry glance

of the afternoon sun picked something out for Henshaw, something he would probably never have noticed except for being in line with the reflected rays. Down below something was gleaming like a silver line.

5

A sound in the office behind him made Henshaw withdraw and he found that Detective-sergeant Willis had returned.

'Nothing to be gleaned from the rest of the people in the building, sir,' he announced glumly. 'They've seen nothing and heard nothing. In fact they seem pretty shocked to discover we're in the building investigating murder. The architects comprise two elderly men — and I don't think they hardly know what a murder is, let alone commit one. The insurance agents comprise one man, an office boy, and a girl typist — rather like it is here. They don't seem to know a thing about it. I'm pretty sure they're not holding anything back.'

'I rather expected it,' Henshaw shrugged. 'It's hardly likely that the murderer would go to the upper floors when his business finished at this one. Incidentally, Willis, what do you make of that?'

The superintendent leaned out of the window again and pointed to the gleaming object below.

'No idea, sir — unless it's a bit of glass from this window when we smashed it. Looks the wrong shape for that, though . . . I'll soon find out.'

He turned actively and left the office. Henshaw removed his head and shoulders from the window and then glanced towards the door as the men arrived with the stretcher to take away the body. He watched them as they completed their task and then, feeling a little more relieved with the corpse out of the way, he began to straighten up the signs of the struggle

He raised the ornamental-backed chair into position and settled it squarely in front of the blotter, where he presumed it normally stood. Then crossing to the armchair he pulled it away from its jammed position against the wall, and picked up the heavy law books. Finally, with a large envelope, he sealed over the gap in the window.

The detective-sergeant returned, holding

in his hand an object shaped like an L, made of thin steel and quite bright, with a curious clip arrangement at each end of it.

Henshaw took it and turned it over in his fingers. 'What the devil is it?'

'My wife uses them, sir,' Willis said, and hesitated. 'For her hair.'

Henshaw, who was also married and therefore thought he knew most of the feminine accoutrements, found himself beaten. 'Go on.'

'Normally these things are straight. The little clips on the ends fix the hair fizzgigs somehow. You know how the womenfolk mess about with their hair. Looks as though some woman must have dropped this in the yard.'

The superintendent turned the bent hairgrip over and over in his fingers and mused. 'Hasn't been out there long anyway,' he said finally. 'It would have rusted otherwise. Only ordinary cheap steel. Well, I'm not going to rack my brains to try and explain this now. Let's take a look at Barridge's office.'

From his pocket he took the envelope containing Barridge's effects, dropped the hairgrip amongst them, and then extracted Barridge's bunch of keys. First he tried all the Yales — there were three — in the lock of Minton's door but none of them fitted.

'Must be one for his home, one for the outer office door, and one for his own office door,' he said finally. 'Let's see what else we can dig up.'

With Willis beside him he left Minton's office and went round to the door of Barridge's room. He had it open in a moment and they entered. Henshaw picked up the brown paper package from the desk and untied the string. Within the paper were three now rather dry cheese sandwiches.

'I'm just wondering, though, why Barridge didn't eat his lunch,' Henshaw said. 'We'd better take these back to the station and get rid of them there.'

Willis folded the paper tightly again and then thrust the lot into his pocket. Next he turned to giving his superior a hand as a search of Barridge's desk — both on the top and in the drawers — was commenced. There did not appear to be anything unusual, nor had the single filing cabinet anything to tell.

'I think we'd better get that janitor up here, Willis, and see what he can tell us. Go and grab him, will you?'

The detective-sergeant returned a few minutes later, with the janitor. The man looked uneasy, glancing up under his eyes and rubbing his hands on a duster.

'You're the janitor here?' Henshaw asked briefly.

'Yes, sir. Baxter's the name. I live on the premises. And if this is about the murder, I don't know anything.'

'Who told you it was murder?'

'Jimmy, the office boy. I sort of forced it out of him. After all, I had a right! I couldn't understand what so many policemen were doing on the premises — '

'All right!' Henshaw looked impatient. 'I'm trying to find out all I can concerning callers. As the janitor you may have seen somebody. So, can you tell me if anybody happened to call on Mr. Barridge between the hours of one and two? The lunch hour?'

'Oh yes, sir — there was a woman.'

'What sort of a woman?' Henshaw enquired. 'Ever see her before?'

'Twice before,' Baxter replied. 'A young, smart, well-set-up lady she is. She came about a quarter-past one and left again at twenty-past.'

'So quickly? Are you sure of the time?'

'Absolutely sure, sir.'

'Did you hear anything? I mean voices, knocking on the door, or anything like that?'

'No, sir — but that isn't anything unusual. I'm pretty pushed away, as you might say, in the back of the building.'

'Her interview only lasted about five minutes then?' Henshaw frowned.

'Must have done,' the janitor agreed. 'I saw her leave and I don't know what happened after that because I went to my lunch at half-past one.'

'Your lunch? But I thought you lived on the premises?'

'I do — but I get my lunch at a little eating-house about fifty yards from here. My wife's out all day charring and I can't be bothered fixing food for myself. So I go out to it.'

'And what time did you get back?'

'Quarter past two, as usual.'

'Then if anybody came between one-thirty and the time when Mr. Minton's office staff returned nobody would know anything about it?'

'I wouldn't, anyway,' the janitor admitted, and waited.

'Can you tell me the name of this woman who called?'

''Fraid not, no. I'm only here to keep the place aired out, stoke the heaters, and deal with loiterers.'

'Let me have a detailed description of the woman, anyway. Take it down. Willis.'

'About twenty-five, blonde, fair amount of make-up — what I could see. Slender build. She had on a fur coat, and one of those latest idiotic sort of hats, like a squashed cauliflower on the side of her 'ead. She'd be about five feet, I'd say.'

'Thanks,' Henshaw said. 'That's all for now, Baxter. I'll let you know if I need you again.'

As the janitor went out, Willis stirred a little. 'Pretty interesting coincidence, sir. The hairgrip and the unknown woman, I mean.'

'There's nothing conclusive about the hairgrip, Willis. Millions of women use them. We are entitled to *suspect* a tie-up certainly, but nothing more. I'm more interested in an interview that only lasted for five minutes. Couldn't have been very important. If it *was* an interview . . . '

Henshaw considered something, then went on:

'There are two other aspects — one, that she merely called to hand something to Barridge and then left again — though I fancy that would take less time than five minutes; and the other, that she couldn't get in the office, Barridge being dead and the door locked, as Sally Higson found it. She waited for a while, got impatient, and then departed. The pity is we haven't much help in that direction since, being buried at the back of the building, the janitor didn't hear anything resembling knocking. Lastly, there is the straight and obvious idea that she walked into the office, stabbed Barridge — '

Henshaw gave an impatient shake of his head.

'What the blazes am I talking about?'

he demanded. 'She couldn't have done. Barridge was in Minton's office with the door locked, and it seems only Minton has the key. That hypothesis just won't work. The person *we* want to interview is Minton himself. If I can't get him I'll see his wife and try and get some information out of her. It's just possible she may know something to start the ball rolling.'

'I wonder why the murderer left the knife in Barridge's back?' Willis asked thoughtfully.

'At the moment, Willis, I've no idea. Before we go any further let's have a look at what sort of stuff Barridge carried around with him. Might tell us something.'

He took the envelope from his pocket, upended it and tipped out the contents on to the desk blotter. There was a heavy gold watch, possibly an heirloom, with an old-fashioned gold chain and fob, fifteen shillings in silver, a still folded white handkerchief, a small penknife with a pearl handle, a star-shaped brooch of some value, made up in small rubies and garnets, a box of matches, pipe, oilskin tobacco pouch, a lump of sealing-wax with a smoke-blackened end, and a small ball of new string. To the assortment Henshaw added the bunch of keys; then from under the heap withdrew a shiny leather wallet.

'Quite a conglomeration, sir,' Willis commented. 'Everything just as you'd expect — except the sealing-wax and the woman's brooch. I can understand the sealing-wax since solicitors use it by the ton, but not the brooch . . . '

'The brooch could have been picked up anywhere,' Henshaw responded. 'It could belong to his wife and is perhaps to be repaired, or something — or else has just been repaired. It could also belong to a woman who has a hat like a squashed cauliflower and is five feet tall. I'm not interested in conjectures. I'll ask Mrs. Barridge if it belongs to her, and if not I'll think further. Now, what have we got in this wallet . . . ?'

He drew out the contents — two one-pound notes, a 'bus contract, a calendar for the year, a card giving the dates of court proceedings, several visiting cards with *William Barridge, 24 Cedar Avenue, Hadlam*, printed upon them, two shillingsworth of stamps, and a registration receipt for a postal packet. Henshaw looked at this last curiously, squinting at the scrawled, hasty writing.

'Today's date,' he commented. 'Stamped from the Hadlam general post office. That's clear enough. But the writing! Hell, why don't these girls in the post office learn to write *properly*? Can you make anything out, Willis?'

'The last word is 'Australia', sir,' Willis said at last, with an air of triumph. 'And the one before it is probably 'Melbourne'. The 'M' is quite clear.'

'That's right enough,' Henshaw agreed, 'but what's the name of the consignee? Looks like — ' He peered earnestly — 'But — Bell — Bill . . . ' He stopped suddenly and gave a brief grin. 'It's Barridge! James Barridge. The full address isn't given. James Barridge, Melbourne, Australia. Since the name is the same it's obviously a relative. I'll ask Mrs. Barridge about it: she should know the person at the Australian end. Not that I expect it to have the remotest connection with the murder except . . . for the sealing-wax and string,' he finished.

'You mean Barridge might have used them for a registered parcel?'

'It's an idea. I know solicitors use sealing wax, but they're hardly in the habit of carrying it about in a jacket pocket. If the wax was used to seal up a parcel we might infer from that that Barridge made the parcel up outside somewhere — perhaps in the post office itself. The new ball of string also seems to suggest that. So it looks as if he tied up a parcel very recently; maybe this morning judging from the registration slip, and used the wax to seal the knots . . . That's an unusual angle and perhaps worth considering. I'll call at the post office whilst I'm out and see if I can get hold of the girl who initialed the slip. She might remember what sort of a parcel was sent off.'

'Can try, sir, anyway . . . though I certainly can't see the connection with the murder.'

'Neither can I at the moment, but you

can never know too much about the movements and actions of a man who has been murdered. I've found that out.' The superintendent got to his feet.

'Quite a few calls ahead of me,' he decided, scooping Barridge's belongings back into the envelope. 'I must call at Minton's home, at Barridge's, on the doctor for his postmortem report — if it's finished — and at the post office. You had better stay here in case Minton should return. If he does, get a statement from him, and from anybody else who might turn up.'

'I will, sir — ' Willis glanced up as there was a knock on the office door. He opened it, admitting P.C. Barton who had been detailed to take Mrs. Barridge to the mortuary in order to identify the body.

'Just in time,' Henshaw commented. 'I was going to 'phone the station for another car. Well, how about Mrs. Barridge? Fix her up at the mortuary?'

'Yes, sir. She identified the body as that of her husband.'

'Good. How did she seem?'

94

'Matter of fact, sir,' the constable answered, 'she looked as though she didn't give a damn. When I'd gently broken the news to her on the doorstep she just stared at me. I was all prepared for her passing out or something like that, but once she'd realized what I was telling her she — she sort of actually looked half pleased. Mind you, sir, I may be wrong, but that's the way it looked.'

'She did, did she?' Henshaw rubbed his chin. 'That's interesting . . . What sort of a woman is she?'

'She's big sir — about fifteen stone. Not very likeable. She said she has three kids, but I didn't see them. At school, I suppose.'

'All right; now I know,' Henshaw said. 'You can drive me to Mr. Minton's home first — the Elms, Shinley Close. You know what to do, Willis. I'll ring up headquarters at intervals as I travel around. If you have anything special that comes in, telephone the message to the station and they can relay it to me. If you get anybody whom you think might be a material witness take them to headquarters and wait for me. Leave Parker on duty in the passage.'

'Leave it to me, sir,' Willis responded.

* * *

In the crowded Roxhome Café in the center of Hadlam a young woman in a fur coat and with a hat like a squashed cauliflower perched on her blonde hair sat sipping tea and playing with biscuits on the plate before her. She was simply killing time — which, in view of the shortage of free tables, was not exactly a generous thing to do.

She had a fellow diner at her table. The only way she could avoid looking straight at him was by looking through him, and this she managed quite successfully. She had just the right length of nose and turn of chin to accomplish it, and it was a pity really that her abilities were wasted on such an earthy specimen, his sole interest seeming to be the manipulation of spaghetti into an overlarge mouth. The young woman had come in here at half-past two after a lingering walk round the shops — and now it was half-past three.

Ultimately, she realized the eyes of her own particular waitress were getting accusing, as the stream of potential customers swelled. She managed to delay a few seconds by touching up her lips from a small compact — an act of bad taste that she considered her spaghetti-eating partner deserved to witness — and then she signalled for her check.

Taking it to the cash desk she paid, left the café, and strolled to Hadlam's main street, hunching her fur coat about her neck against the razor breath of the wind. She walked along to Fenway's Emporium and killed another hour looking at articles she had no intention of purchasing.

At four-thirty she made her way to the street again, walking slowly along the pavement and finally turned into the amusement arcade and so through to Parkhurst Street. At Chertsey House she hurried up the three stone steps of the Georgian portico and then up the bare staircase to the first floor. Then stopped.

The sight of a massive police constable

loomed — waiting.

'Somebody you wish to see, madam?' he asked, quite affably.

'Why, yes . . . ' The woman had a quick, intelligent, and melodious voice. 'I want to see Mr. Barridge. He's — he's the head clerk at — at Minton's . . . '

'What was it about, madam?' The police constable waited in perfect respect for the answer, studying the woman meanwhile. She was definitely good-looking with a straight nose, pointed chin, and clear grey-blue eyes. Her blonde hair, he noted, was coiffured and even the idiotic hat did not seem to mar it.

'Why should I tell you?' the woman asked suddenly; and that she possessed intelligence was now confirmed. 'What's the matter here? Why are *you* here?'

'I have no authority to answer that question, madam. Maybe you had better see the detective-sergeant.'

'*Detective-sergeant?*' There was utter bewilderment in the woman's voice — but nonetheless she obeyed the slight motion of the constable's hand as he ushered her into the main enquiry office.

Willis was seated at Sally Higson's desk, passing his time typing out the statements he had so far taken down in shorthand. As the woman was shown in he looked up quickly.

'The lady just arrived, sir,' the constable explained. 'To see Mr. Barridge. I thought you'd like a word with her.'

'Thanks,' Willis responded, and the constable went out.

The woman advanced slowly, gazing at Willis as with a faint smile he got to his feet and drew up a chair for her.

'What is all this *about*?' The woman seated herself, and put her handbag on the desk.

'My superior, Superintendent Henshaw, is out at the moment,' Willis explained. 'I'm deputizing for him. There's nothing to be alarmed about, I assure you. There's been some trouble. I'm afraid I shall have to ask you your reason for wishing to see Mr. Barridge.'

'How on earth can my business with Mr. Barridge concern *you*? Where *is* Mr. Barridge? What's happened to him?'

The detective-sergeant could either

reveal the nature of the crime or suppress it, according to his estimation of the person concerned. In this case he said quietly:

'Mr. Barridge was murdered about half-past one today.'

'Mur — dered!' The woman's eyes took on a brief frozen look of real fear; then the stare of bewilderment returned.

'Since the facts will be in the Press by tonight there is no point in my withholding information from you — naturally we have to question everybody with the remotest personal or business connection with Mr. Barridge . . . You will be the lady who called about one-twenty today?'

She started slightly. 'How did you know that?'

'The janitor saw you arrive. And depart.'

'Oh!' She pulled off her right glove, and then for no reason at all started putting it on again. Willis watched the performance with dour detachment.

'I'd be glad of your name and address,' he said.

'You can have it with pleasure. I'm

Jennifer Carr. My address is Flat Seven, Lexhall Mansions, north Hadlam. I've — I've a little place there. I live alone.' She gave a fleeting smile that revealed perfect teeth.

Willis wrote down the name and address and nodded. '*Miss* Jennifer Carr, of course? Living alone?'

'Oh, no. I'm married.'

'Mrs. Carr, then.' Willis had no expression. 'Sorry, madam. Well, to return to my first question — What was the nature of your business with Mr. Barridge?'

'It was about my divorce. Mr. Barridge has it — I mean *had* it — in hand.'

'Was it for the purpose of this divorce that you called here on two other occasions?'

Though it was evident the woman wondered how the fact was known she nodded acquiescence. 'That was the reason. Mr. Barridge was pretty certain he would be able to arrange the divorce for me.'

'Was Mr. Minton of the same opinion?'

'I don't know. I've never seen Mr. Minton yet. Mr. Barridge said that Mr. Minton does not take matters in hand until the preliminaries have been arranged — and Mr. Barridge always attended to the preliminaries. I didn't argue the point, though I must say I thought once or twice I would have liked to have dealt with the head of the firm.'

'I see. So you came at about twenty-past one to discuss your divorce. Didn't you know it was lunch-time for the staff?'

'That hardly concerned me, sergeant. Mr. Barridge telephoned me to come over for one-fifteen — so I came. I saw no reason to question the time of the invitation.'

Willis made a note. 'He telephoned you? About what time?'

'Oh — er — ' The woman reflected. 'It must have been about one o'clock, or just after. I know it only allowed me time to dash into my hat and coat and catch the 'bus to come straight here. I had to interrupt my lunch to do it.'

'And when you got here?'

'To my annoyance, I found the place locked up. I rattled the door and knocked, but nobody answered. Finally, after hanging round for about five minutes, I left. With Mr. Barridge having 'phoned me I naturally expected to find him in. I could only assume that something very urgent had called him away and there had been no time to let me know . . . I wish I had known about the janitor. He might have been able to tell me something.'

'And then later on you decided to return?'

'Yes. I chose the time when I have been before — about quarter to five. It always seemed to be the period when Mr. Barridge was least busy. I've been killing time since half-past one, and now — '

Jennifer Carr stopped and began working her right glove slowly off again. Willis reflected, wondering about two things — a star-shaped brooch and a hairgrip. Knowing his job, however, he was perfectly aware that this was not the time to mention either of them. In any case the superintendent would probably want to handle that tricky bit of work himself — but there was nothing to prevent a study of the woman's hair, casually. With this idea in mind Willis got to his feet and first ambled to the window, staring through the steamy glass on to the back yards.

'How long have you been suing for divorce, Mrs. Carr?' he asked. 'Arranging things through Mr. Barridge, I mean?'

'About a fortnight. Sometimes we discussed here; sometimes outside. On two other occasions I met Mr. Barridge after office hours to clear up some trivial point or other. On each occasion he met me and we went to the Roxhome Café.'

'Oh, I see.' Willis wandered past the woman, from the rear, and took a brief glance at her marvelously contrived hair. He tensed as he noted skillfully concealed, as many as four of the hairgrips that in the normal shape, duplicated the one he had found in the yard.

'And your husband, Mrs. Carr?' he asked. 'Doesn't he come here, too, for his side of the divorce story?'

'He can't.' The woman turned her head slightly to follow Willis's course back to the desk.

'You see he's in Melbourne. Australia, you know.'

6

The Melbourne reference gave the detective-sergeant a momentary feeling of confusion. Events in Australia couldn't be related to a murder in Chertsey House, Hadlam, surely?

'Melbourne?' Willis repeated casually. 'How does that come about? Did you once live there and then came back here — or what?'

'My husband deserted me after we had been married for six months,' she said frankly. 'That was two years ago. Quite recently I had a letter from him in which he stated that he was in Melbourne and that I could start divorce proceedings if I wanted. Nothing wrong in that, is there? Mr. Barridge had all the details.'

'I see.' Willis's eyes strayed to the door of Barridge's office. 'Excuse me a moment, Mrs. Carr,' he added, and following up a notion he went into Barridge's office and opened the filing cabinet, walking his fingers through the 'A' and 'B' files until he came to 'C'.

There was no sign of a file under the name of Jennifer Carr. On the off-chance that there might have been an error he ploughed through a bulky 'Miscellaneous' file and achieved precisely nothing. Annoyed, he looked about him, in the drawers of the desk, all of which were now unlocked, but there was not the remotest suggestion of a Carr file anywhere.

Thoughtfully he came back into the main office. The woman seemed calmer now as she watched him.

'I suppose,' Willis said, settling at the desk again and making a note, 'the case is under your own name?'

'Of course.'

Willis wrote: '*No file for Carr*,' and asked: 'What is your husband's name, Mrs. Carr?'

'Centinel Carr. Centinel — spelt with a 'C'. His mother was a Miss Centinel. A bit unusual, I know.'

Willis felt himself floundering. If there was no file for Carr, as surely there ought to be in a solicitor's office, it suggested that no case for Carr was in existence. Which, for all her seeming frankness, made Mrs. Carr seem like a barefaced liar.

'What is your husband's address, madam?' Willis asked at last.

'What's he got to do with it? After all, he can hardly be connected with the murder of Mr. Barridge, now can he? Six thousand miles away!'

'I'd like to know just the same,' Willis persisted. 'We shall have to get in touch with him if only to verify the story of the divorce.'

'In case I'm not speaking the truth?' Jennifer Carr smiled cynically for a moment. 'His address is two thirty-six North Elizabeth Street, Melbourne. That's the only address I know, contained in his letter which reached me a fortnight or so ago. Since he said I could have a divorce and he wouldn't contest it, I decided I would — suing for desertion, just the same. Mr. Barridge agreed with me that I had a good case.'

'Thank you.' Willis made a note of the address, then said formally: 'I think the superintendent would like a word with you, Mrs. Carr. I think you had better accompany me to headquarters.'

'Are you trying to tell me I'm under arrest? I haven't *done* anything!'

Willis picked up the reports he had partly typed. 'There is no question of arrest or even of anything approaching it. I am only following out instructions. As I told you, we want the fullest details regarding everybody even slightly connected with Mr. Barridge. So, if you will come along?'

Jennifer Carr picked up her handbag. 'How long is it likely to take? I have an appointment this evening.'

'The superintendent shouldn't be long.' Willis opened the door, left instructions with the constable to remain on guard, and then accompanied the woman down the dreary staircase.

★   ★   ★

As he was driven to Shinley Close and the home of Henry Minton the superintendent mused over the notes he had made so far.

Standish: I often wondered how Mr. Barridge stood for it. (Only one person has the key to Minton's door — Minton himself.)

Standish: Every morning Mr. Barridge used to have the keys to the strong-room (entire bunch belonging to Minton).

Miss Higson: I always considered Barridge to be a bit stupid, but particularly sharp this morning.

Jimmy: (quoting Miss Higson): Things would be much pleasanter in the office without Mr. Barridge.

Henshaw turned the page and inspected the plan he had made of the office. He considered it from every angle — but finally he was forced to the conclusion that at this stage at least there was nothing which conceivably made sense, and to kill a man just because he had been 'stupid' was utterly illogical. Murder required desperate incentive.

'And often a woman's behind it,' Henshaw muttered, and the constable at the wheel glanced at him enquiringly.

'Just thinking aloud. Many crimes can be traced to the influence of a woman.'

To his notes Heashaw added *Cherchez la femme* and then put the book away as the constable turned the car into Shinley Close. The superintendent was surprised at the sight of the residence owned by Henry Minton: a massive, old-fashioned house standing in its own extensive grounds, separated by an aloof distance from the much less pretentious abodes of Shinley Close. It was the kind of home one would expect of a millionaire industrialist. Evidently Henry Minton either made charges far above those sanctioned by the Law Society, or else he had outside sources of income.

'Wait here,' Henshaw instructed, as he got out of the car. Pushing open the tall wrought-iron double gate he walked up the long, elm-lined drive to the front door, and pressed the bell in the porch.

Presently a spruce, alert-eyed maid opened the door. 'Yes?' she asked uneasily, as she saw the official uniform.

Henshaw identified himself and added, 'Is Mrs. Minton at home?'

'I — er — that is, I'd better see — '

'What is it, Susan?' enquired a quiet,

cultured voice from the big hall, as a genteel looking woman of middle age, exquisitely dressed, came into Henshaw's line of vision. She had a round, once-pretty face, and a hairstyle becoming her years.

'I saw you coming up the drive, superintendent,' she explained. 'I just can't imagine — But do come in.' To the maid she added, 'That will be all, Susan.'

Henshaw, uniform-cap in hand, followed the woman through a broad, tastefully-furnished hall and into a well-appointed drawing-room. He found himself motioned to an armchair, and the woman seated herself on the chesterfield nearby.

'Now, superintendent? Have I been transgressing the law by parking my car on the wrong side of the road, or what?'

'This has nothing to do with you, madam — except I'm hoping you may be able to help me. I really wanted to see your husband, but I understand he is out of town?'

The woman shrugged. 'He may be. I don't know. I'm afraid I have not the least idea how my husband conducts his business affairs, or where he goes. He never tells me and I never ask him. He's always going off somewhere, but in a busy man I suppose that it is only natural.'

Henshaw had the impression that she did not particularly care *what* her husband did.

'Why did you wish to see him?' she asked quietly. 'Or can't you tell me?'

'In this case I can,' Henshaw answered. 'His chief clerk, Mr. Barridge, has been murdered.'

'Murdered? Mr. *Barridge* . . . '

'Naturally, since Mr. Minton is head of the firm I have to get in touch with him. I've been told that he left the office about quarter-past ten this morning and nobody seems to know where he is or when he'll be back.'

'I'm afraid I can't help you, superintendent. But I'm sure he won't be away long. When he left here this morning he made no reference to a long absence, nor had he any bags packed. He should be back this evening. But what a dreadful thing about Mr. Barridge!' she broke off. 'I just can't believe it.'

Henshaw rose. 'I quite understand, madam. Sorry I had to bother you.'

'It will be a terrible shock to my husband. Just as it has been for me.'

'You knew Mr. Barridge?' Henshaw asked.

'Very well indeed, in a business sense, that is. I often saw him when I had reason to call on my husband at the office. He was always the soul of respect, and for some reason I used to feel sorry for him. A . . . womanly instinct perhaps. He was quiet and reserved — perhaps too much so to suit my husband.'

'Oh?'

The woman smiled enigmatically. 'My husband has a most aggressive personality, superintendent. Such people are rarely tolerant towards those less aggressive.'

Henshaw sensed that the comment was two-edged. Aloud he said: 'When your husband returns perhaps you won't mind asking him to ring me up at the police station? Hadlam six nine. If he prefers to call personally, so much the better.'

'I'll see he gets the message,' the

woman promised, and with this Henshaw took his departure and returned to the car.

'Take me to Dr. Paget's,' he instructed the constable driving the car. 'He may have finished his post-mortem by now and I want to be knowing something.'

★ ★ ★

Dr. Paget had just returned to his home from making the post-mortem at the mortuary and, following a belated lunch, was catching up on lost time in his dispensary when Henshaw was shown in to him.

'Oh, hello, super! Come rooting after that body of Barridge's, I suppose?'

'That's the general idea.'

Paget put down a prescription. 'I've got all the facts for you. The report is on my desk in the study. I was going to send someone over with it during the afternoon because I know it's pretty urgent. And in my opinion it's quite an interesting case.

'The knife,' he went on, 'pierced the

114

body just below the left scapula, as I'd thought, and then penetrated the muscular wall of the heart from the back, finishing up in the right auricle. There's a clear trail where the knife entered, and although I didn't see the length of the blade I imagine it was about eight inches long. Right?'

'Right,' Henshaw agreed. 'Eight inches exactly — a pretty abnormal length in a dagger: almost makes it a small sword. The blade, by the way, was double-edged.'

'I gathered that.'

'It also had a broad hilt crosspiece,' Henshaw added. 'Or rather a long one — three inches. The blade was certainly long enough to have pierced the heart from the back. I suppose death must have been instantaneous?'

'By all the laws of materia-medica, yes. I say that,' Paget added, 'because the oddest things happen sometimes. It takes far more than one would think to bring death. For all practical purposes, however, you may assume that death was instantaneous when the heart was pierced.

There are, though, two interesting factors in connection with the *direction* of the blade thrust.'

Henshaw became immediately attentive.

'The lip of the knife wound seems to have been caused by the knife found in the body,' Paget went on. 'Barridge evidently dropped dead and didn't move afterwards — which helped me a lot in my examination. When the body shifts position at the moment of receiving injury the parts get twisted and displaced. However, you'll find all that covered in my report. What I want to mention specially is that the right hand lip of the wound is oddly spragged. Now that's odd! A very sharp knife does not always produce a clean cut, of course, but in this case the wound *should* have been clean cut because the knife struck home in an absolutely straight line. Its path was not diagonal, or twisted, a fact that you may consider important. In other words, it entered exactly at right angles to Barridge's body, just below the scapula, and followed a straight line into the back of his heart. Yet the right-hand lip is slightly twisted back as though a brief but violent tugging occurred. It's an aspect I don't quite understand.'

'Definitely queer,' Henshaw admitted, musing.

'I've checked up on the various sorts of wounds left by knives in all manner of attacks, yet I haven't been able to alight on one which explains this away. Even Hans Gross has nothing to say on it although he covered most angles in the field in his chapter on stabbing weapons.'

'Entered at right angles, eh? Can you show me exactly how?'

'Certainly. Just stand straight for a moment. Now, I point my finger here.' Henshaw felt it prod just below his left shoulder blade. 'And it — the blade — goes straight into your body, parallel with the floor, and ends up in the back of your heart. That should make a clean-cut wound — since a double-edged knife was employed — with a slightly elliptical slit in the body. In Barridge's body we have that — *and* the right hand lip-sprag I've mentioned.'

Henshaw frowned. 'I don't understand

the reason for the sprag, Doctor: it's out of my line. What also puzzles me is the manner of stabbing. You'd think that anybody stabbing a man would drive the blade in diagonally — down and slant-wise, and if the heart was aimed at you'd expect the breast to be the target, not the back.'

'Yes . . . I agree.' Paget smiled slightly. 'That, though, is your field, not mine. There's one other thing, not relative to the case, but you'd better know of it. Barridge was suffering from advanced endocarditis.'

'What's that?' Henshaw asked.

'Inflammation of the endocardium or membrane of the heart. I noticed it as I made the p.m. It's very often the outcome of severe rheumatism at some time in life. If taken in time it can be cured, but Barridge had *not* taken it in time. Had he lived he would have had plenty of trouble with that heart of his before long. In fact I don't think it would be too much of an exaggeration to say that he would probably have died pretty soon anyway. Endocarditis is serious, once it gets a hold

— and sudden. One minute you're here, and the next — gone. Countless deaths from heart failure are due to endocarditis ... As I say, I don't know if it matters, but you might as well know.'

'Thanks,' Henshaw said, and made a note of the technical term. 'Anything else?'

'None that I can think of. The body's still in the mortuary where I presume it will remain until after the inquest?'

'Right,' Henshaw agreed. 'Perhaps you'll send your report on as usual, then? Oh — may I use your 'phone?' Paget nodded.

Henshaw got through to his headquarters. The sergeant-in-charge immediately put him on to Willis, nor did Willis waste any time in announcing that Jennifer Carr was waiting for him, and added the details.

'Good!' Henshaw exclaimed. 'I'll come over right away and attend to Mrs. Barridge and the post office later on. This may be important.'

★ ★ ★

In ten minutes he was back at headquarters and Willis followed him into the private office. 'Well, where is she?' Henshaw asked.

'In my office, sir, and getting pretty well worked up over being kept waiting. She says she has an appointment or something this evening and thinks you might show her a bit more consideration.'

'If she will get herself mixed up in a murder case she'll have to take all that goes with it.'

'Yes, sir. Here's what she's said up to now — and here are the other statements. I managed to type them out.'

Henshaw settled at his desk and put aside the statements of Minton's office staff to concentrate on Jennifer Carr's. 'Tell Parker — he's in the enquiry office — to take these round to the various people concerned and get them signed and initialed in the usual way . . . Mmmm, so this is what Mrs. Carr has to say, is it? Very interesting.'

As Henshaw read the report carefully, Willis added: 'I haven't put on that, sir, that she uses hairgrips similar to the bent one we found in the yard.'

'I'll remember it anyway,' Henshaw responded, lowering the sheet. 'Bring her in, Willis.'

Henshaw got to his feet with a smile as the good-looking young lady in the fur coat and absurd hat came into the office.

'Good afternoon, Mrs. Carr — or I should say good evening since it's getting near six o'clock — '

'Of which I'm well aware!' she interrupted.

'Sorry you had to wait. Have a chair, please.'

Henshaw settled her comfortably, and went back to his desk. Willis settled at the small table near the window, prepared to take further notes.

'What do you *want* with me?' she demanded abruptly. 'All this is most — embarrassing, and I've told the sergeant already that I have better things to do.'

'I can appreciate your feelings,' Henshaw sympathized, 'but unfortunately we have to follow routine . . . I have here a statement of your information given to the sergeant, Mrs. Carr, and I'd like a few embellishments.'

'Well — all right, but please be quick.'

'Can you tell me why it was necessary for Mr. Barridge to discuss business with you outside the office, in the Roxhome Café? Was the matter of your divorce so extraordinary that it could not be discussed in Mr. Barridge's office?'

'We just did, that's all.' A delicate touch of colour rose behind the rouge on Jennifer Carr's cheeks and Henshaw was not slow to notice it.

'There must have been *some* reason for departing from normal procedure,' Henshaw insisted. 'Murder has been done, Mrs. Carr. Any secrets anybody might have had — either you or the office staff — no longer count for a thing. I cannot force you to speak, of course, but I would point out that you were the only person seen near the office at the approximate time Mr. Barridge was murdered.'

'It's — it's all so perfectly ridiculous!' the woman exclaimed abruptly, working off her right glove fiercely. 'Well, you see — Mr. Barridge took a fancy to me. He even tried to make love to me! I didn't know what was coming, but that was the *real* purpose behind the after office hours business meetings. He sort of led me into it.'

'As a married man, he should have known better; and, if I may say so, so should you!'

'I *told* him he should know better. I think that knowing of my impending divorce and my consequent freedom he had some idea in mind about separating from his wife and marrying me — if I would have had him.'

'And what did you do?'

'I'm afraid I laughed at him, and repulsed his advances. From my point of view it was *too* ridiculous. Of course there seemed every possibility that I would get my divorce, but even so . . . Well, I'm young — attractive, I think. What on earth would I want with a meek and mild balding man of approaching middle age, and nothing to offer beyond the salary of a clerk? I told him as much. In fact I told him that my aim was to find a rich young man with reasonably good looks. Not,'

Jennifer Carr added demurely, 'that I'm short of money. My father left me well provided for, but one may just as well have more.'

'How did Barridge take it?' Henshaw asked.

'I don't quite know.' The woman looked thoughtful. 'I think it was a shock to him, though. Still, since he never referred to the incident again. I assumed that he'd forgotten all about it. I know I did, right away. From that point on I insisted that our meetings should be purely for business, and in his office.'

'Thanks for being so frank, Mrs. Carr.' The superintendent made a note. 'I understand that desertion is the ground for your divorce?'

'Yes. My husband left me three years ago and went to Australia.'

'And the letter your husband sent you from Australia was the first intimation you had received that he was in that country?'

'The very first. I had thought he might be dead. When he first vanished I asked the police to help me find him, but nothing came of it.'

'And this Australian letter was considered by Mr. Barridge to be sufficient ground for suing for divorce?'

'Yes,' the woman assented. 'Chiefly because in the letter he *asked* me to sue for divorce and added that he would not contest it. That, and the first letters I wrote to my husband at the time of our engagement were considered by Mr. Barridge to be all that was needed.'

'Letters?' Hensgaw looked interested. 'You mean love letters, I suppose?'

'Yes. There are three of them.' She gave an embarrassed little smile. 'You know how it is in such matters. When Mr. Barridge said he would like all the evidence he could get on my first amorous inclinations towards my husband I decided to let him — Mr. Barridge — see them. He told me they were just what he needed, that they would prove that I had been deeply in love with my husband and that, for no reason at all, he had just walked out.'

'Then these letters were in the care of Mr. Barridge before he was murdered?'

'I presume so.'

Henshaw raised his eyes a trifle and saw that Willis was shaking his head deliberately and pointing a thumb downwards. Henshaw looked at the line on the report that said, '*No file for Carr*' and considered for a space.

'If you have nothing more to ask me, superintendent, I really would like to go. I have to change and prepare for the evening. As a matter of fact,' she added, 'I'm going to meet a young man whom I hope may fill the bill very nicely when eventually I'm free.'

Henshaw smiled and stood up. 'By all means carry on, Mrs. Carr, and I'm sorry I had to detain you.' He opened the door for her. 'I'll get in touch with you again if I need — Oh, you are on the telephone?'

'Of course I am. How else do you imagine Mr. Barridge 'phoned me this dinner time?'

Henshaw knew perfectly well that Barridge had 'phoned, but there was another aspect which interested him. 'I take it the telephone is in your own flat? Is it a dial or ordinary telephone?'

'Dial.' Jennifer Carr frowned. 'Where is

this leading, superintendent?'

Henshaw smiled. 'The telephone at Minton's is also on the dial system. You received the call alone, and presumably Mr. Barridge was also alone when he made it. Since he is dead there is only your word for it. A dial call through the automatic exchange cannot be checked.'

'Are you trying to say that he didn't call me?' the woman asked shortly.

'I believe you,' Henshaw answered. 'And thank you, Mrs. Carr. I'll have your statement finished and sent over for signing before very long.'

The woman went off huffily down the corridor. Henshaw closed the door quietly and returned to his desk.

'Altogether, sir,' Willis remarked, 'it seems that you and I between us have got all the information we can out of that lady, and unless I miss my guess she isn't anybody's fool either. There's just one thing you missed out, though. You didn't ask her about the brooch — and about the hairgrip, too.'

'All in good time, Willis. That woman has steeled herself so much to the unexpected that to spring the brooch now might only produce a negative result. I'll try later when she has had time to settle down a little — and also when I'm quite sure the brooch doesn't belong to anybody else, Mrs. Barridge for instance. As to the hairgrip, we'll come to that in time . . .'

'Her story sounds convincing enough to me,' Willis commented. 'I can quite imagine old Barridge falling for her as he did. Henpecked, I'd say, and always being put on.'

'Yes . . . always being put on,' Henshaw agreed absently. 'That, up to now, has been the predominant factor throughout . . . Have some tea sent in, Willis. It just occurs to me that it's about time we had some.'

The detective-sergeant nodded and relayed his instructions to the sergeant in the enquiry office. After a while the nearby café sent in the necessary, and over the cups and sandwiches Henshaw and Willis brooded some more.

'Nobody would kill a man just because he happened to be weak-kneed,' Henshaw said presently. 'A far stronger reason must have existed. I haven't bothered myself unduly about it because so far I have not talked to Mr. Minton: I'm hoping he will get us a good way farther on the road. Meanwhile here's one hypothesis to be going on with:

'Minton returned unexpectedly at lunchtime and sent for Barridge to come into his private office. There, for reasons we don't know, there was a struggle and Barridge got the worst of it with a knife in the back. Minton left, slamming his office door, and the outer office door. Being Yales, the locks both locked themselves. Minton's 'going away' alibi might have been prearranged: we'll see about that later. He would know whether the janitor would be at lunch or not and also when the staff — except Barridge — would be away. There it is, clear as daylight, only a certain factor knocks the bottom out of it.'

'And what's that, sir? Unless you mean the bent hair-grip?'

'No. That could have been put there as a red herring. I mean the fact that Barridge's office door was locked. Why?

What reason could he have had for locking his office if the boss only wanted to see him? As far as he knew, he would not be with his employer very long, and would then go back into his own office — so I repeat: why lock the door? And a draught isn't the explanation because the window we found closed and locked, and anyway nobody but a damned fool would open it on an icy day like this. Unless Minton locked it, which still makes me ask why. He might lock his own door and that of the outer office. Quite logical — to delay discovery of the body. But why Barridge's?'

Willis admitted that he could not see the sense of it.

'I wonder,' Henshaw said, musing, 'how tall Minton is? I'm thinking of what Dr. Paget had to say — concerning the post-mortem made on Barridge. It might help if we knew Minton's height. Barridge was about five feet seven. Only a much smaller person would strike him in a straight line, as happened in this case. The alternative is that Barridge was lying face down on the floor when he got the blow, but even then there would surely be a somewhat diagonal tendency in the striking movement. Maybe I can find out about Minton,' he finished, and pulled the telephone to him.

Presently he was speaking to the janitor at Chertsey House, and the answer he got to his question made him compress his lips.

'About five feet ten or six feet,' he announced. 'If he and Barridge were standing Minton would strike downwards at a slant — and surely he would aim right at the heart instead of, so to speak, going in the back way? Then there is that sideways pull to be accounted for, and the knife being left in the body. Unless, since Minton realized that everybody in the office was acquainted with his paperknife, he saw nothing to be gained by taking it away and disposing of it. For one thing, in removing it, blood might have got on to his clothes and been traced later to Barridge's blood group ... Something fishy somewhere, Willis.'

'Looks like it, sir. Do you think there is anything significant in that ailment

Barridge had? Endo — something or other.'

'Endocarditis? I don't know ... '
Henshaw got to his feet and glanced at the clock. 'This will never do! The post office closes soon and I want to enquire about this registration receipt. Got to get as much information as we can for when the Chief descends to see how we're progressing.'

'The alibis of the office staff have still to be checked too, sir.'

'Mmmm — that's right.' Henshaw stood weighing his course of action. 'I also want to have another look at Barridge's own office because it seems unbelievable to me that the case of Jennifer Carr isn't recorded. It *must* be! Or else it may be in the general office. Won't be in Minton's, presumably, because he hadn't handled the business. Which seems another queer thing.'

'I've looked, but didn't find anything.'

'I'm not doubting it, but you didn't have time to look very far. Tell you what we'll do. It shouldn't take you above an hour to check the alibi of Standish at the

Crescent Café, and that of Miss Higson and the office boy at their homes. Do that and then meet me at Minton's office. I'll go there after calling at the post office. I'll also have to arrange a relief constable at Minton's, too.'

'See you later then, sir,' Willis agreed.

7

Henshaw arrived at the registration counter of the post-office and his official uniform had the effect of making the green-eyed girl behind the grille come to swifter attention than usual.

''Evening, miss,' Henshaw said gruffly. 'Were you on duty here between the time the place opened this morning and half-past one?'

'Yes. I went off duty at two and came on again at five-thirty. Something wrong?'

'Not exactly. I just want you to try and remember something. Can you recall what *this* applied to?' Henshaw handed the registration receipt under the grille. 'It is your writing, isn't it?' he asked rather dryly.

'Yes — and my initials. But — ' The girl shook her head at length. 'I'm so sorry, Inspector, I can't remember what it applies to. I've dealt with dozens of registered letters and parcels today, to all parts of the world. I can remember about seven to Australia.'

She turned and began a hurried search through the carbon receipts of the registration book.

'No — ten,' she amended. 'With this being the general post-office I get such a lot of people to deal with. Unless I am asked particularly to watch for something I'm afraid I — well, just don't.'

Henshaw sighed and took the registration slip back. 'Have all the registered parcels and letters been sent off?' he asked.

'Er — ' The girl turned and glanced at the clock. 'Yes half an hour ago.' She faced him again through the meshwork. 'Anything that comes in before we close will go first thing tomorrow. Whatever it was it is on its way by now.'

'So it seems. Thanks, anyway.'

Disappointed, Henshaw left the post-office and walked the short distance to Chertsey House. The janitor let him in at the main street door, and he found that his instructions at the police station had been carried out and a fresh constable had now come on duty. He gave a respectful salute.

'Sergeant Willis arrived yet?' Henshaw enquired.

'Not yet, sir.'

'When he does come, send him in to me.'

Henshaw went into the general office, and switched on the lights. He began a systematic search for the file for Jennifer Carr.

His first move was to the still open strong room, and with infinite thoroughness he went through the stiff oblong envelopes bound in pink tape, the written title on the labels serving to guide him — but though he inspected every shelf he found no trace of what he wanted, nor was there apparently anything in the locked boxes to judge from the inscriptions on the outsides.

Next he tried the filing cabinets in the general office, without result. It was the same in Minton's office, as far as the filing cabinets were concerned. The safe was another matter. Might be something in it, once Minton had opened it. The desk drawers, to Henshaw's annoyance, were locked, and since he had no authority to open them he resolved to have Minton over at the earliest moment and lay the entire office wide open.

He was feeling pretty disgruntled when Willis arrived.

'Took me longer than I'd expected, sir,' he apologized. 'I've checked up on Miss Higson and Jimmy and they had lunch at home all right. In regard to Standish, though, nobody seems to remember anything about him. I tried some of the waitresses and the girl in the cash-desk but they couldn't help me a bit.'

'Standish was afraid of that,' Henshaw said. 'It doesn't make him guilty of dirty work, but we'll have to keep an eye on him until we've proved what he said.'

'Additionally,' Willis said, 'I asked both Miss Higson and Jimmy — separately — if they had ever heard of a divorce case or file connected with the name of Carr. They said 'no', and it wasn't just a snap answer. Sally Higson had some vague idea about it being mentioned when somebody called. That would be when

Mrs. Carr herself came, I take it.'

'Confoundedly odd!' Henshaw muttered. 'One just can't conduct a divorce case without giving the clerks some inkling. Miss Higson should surely have typed letters or had some sort of connection with the affair. And that nosy office boy would root out anything!'

'All of which,' Willis said, 'makes Mrs. Carr figure rather dubiously in the whole business. She admitted that Barridge made a pass at her. Perhaps he got *too* attentive and so she settled his hash. Maybe it was . . . impulse.'

'It's possible, of course, but how did the body get in here? Minton is the sole possessor of the key.'

'Well, we know that Barridge had the whole bunch of keys every day to unlock the strong room door. He could have had a duplicate key of this office made from a wax impression. Easily done — even while he was supposedly rooting about in the strong room. Then if he had a key made, he could get in and out of here at will, boss or no boss!'

'That's a thought, Willis. Damned if it

isn't: and I'd missed it ... Any other good notions?'

'Well, sir, let's suppose the outer office was actually *open* when Mrs. Carr arrived at lunchtime. Barridge was waiting for her, having 'phoned her. He knew the rest of the staff would be absent, and hadn't bothered with his lunch because he knew she was coming ... All right, in comes Mrs. Carr. Mr. Barridge comes into this office of Mr. Minton's — for how could Mrs. Carr know that only Minton had the key to it? Barridge then got fresh. She, defending herself, stabbed him in the back. She is five feet tall. He was five feet seven. The blow would be more or less horizontal than diagonal from somebody seven inches less in height. Then she dashed out in blind panic, slamming every door, including Barridge's, as she went ... maybe with the idea of slowing things up when it came to discovering the body. The only thing I'm doubtful about is if it could all be done in five minutes. Maybe the janitor was a bit wrong in his time and that would account for it. Also a lot would depend on how soon Barridge became unpleasant and how quickly Mrs. Carr reacted and stabbed him ... Of course it makes you wonder why she came back as large as life afterwards — unless it was sheer curiosity.'

'And dangerous curiosity,' Henshaw commented. 'But why should Barridge chose this office instead of his own? Might he not have realized that it was a dangerous move with such a wicked paperknife on the desk here?'

'Possible he never thought about that, sir. As for this office ... It's more sumptuous than Barridge's. Maybe he wanted to show that he had the complete run of the place. Men will do crazy things sometimes to impress a woman.'

'*Cherchez la femme*,' Henshaw muttered, then added: 'In that case a duplicate key to this office should have been amongst Barridge's effects — but it wasn't. I tried all the Yales. Remember?'

The detective-sergeant nodded moodily. 'Which completely scotches my bright idea, doesn't it?'

'You did well.' Henshaw told him, smiling. 'Maybe there's a good deal more truth in what you've said than you think. Incidentally, does the hairgrip tie up with your hypothesis?'

'I don't know. If Jennifer Carr committed the murder, I can't imagine her being such a fool as to throw a clue like that hairgrip into the yard. And it could not have got there by accident. As to the L-shape, I'm completely licked. I've been wondering if perhaps it's a blind lead, if perhaps it really belongs to the janitor's wife and she happened to drop it recently whilst in the yard.'

'Hardly in the shape of an L, though,' Henshaw answered — and for a long moment a thought had possession of him. Then he stirred actively. 'I've Barridge's office to look through yet for signs of Mrs. Carr's divorce. Better give me a hand or we'll be stuck on this job all night . . .'

★ ★ ★

At 7.40, fifteen minutes late, the London train steamed into Hadlam station, and amidst the deafening hiss of escaping steam and clangor of milk-cans the weary-looking travelers tumbled out of the steamy warmth of the compartments into an arctic blast of wind. As they went through the barriers, probably the least unhappy-looking passenger of the lot was Henry Minton.

Without luggage or briefcase, he was dressed as in the morning in black homburg and overcoat, his bulbous-ended nose slightly redder than usual as the wind caught it. He handed up his ticket, and then, humming genially to himself, walked out to his private car waiting at the entrance.

The chauffeur saluted promptly. "Evening, sir. Home?'

'No, better drop me at the office first, Grant. I'll see if any correspondence has turned up. Barridge may have left some kind of note for me. If it's very important I can still attend to it tonight.'

'Very good, sir.'

As he was driven through Hadlam's centre towards Parkhurst Street Minton had the look of a man who has brought off a successful business venture. His complacency soon vanished, however, when arriving at the first floor of Chertsey House — after the janitor admitted him — he beheld in the stair light the looming figure of the guardian constable.

'What the devil are you doing here?' Minton demanded.

'Somebody you wish to see, sir?' the constable enquired.

'*See?*' Minton hooted the word. 'I'm Henry Minton! What's this all about? What right have you to be outside my premises?'

'Maybe you'd better see the superintendent, sir. He's in the office.'

Half in anger, half in curiosity, Minton strode into the general office, just as Henshaw and Willis were coming out of Barridge's room following a fruitless search for traces of the Carr divorce.

'You'll be the superintendent, I suppose?' Minton asked sourly, looking at Henshaw. 'I'm Henry Minton. What do you imagine you're doing here?'

'Glad to see you, Mr. Minton.' Henshaw took no more than passing notice of Minton's anger. 'I've been wanting to get in touch with you. Your staff couldn't help me, and your wife hadn't the least idea of your whereabouts.'

'Why should she have? Why didn't you ask Barridge? I told *him* where I was going. I told him to keep it to himself, but the police is a different matter. And look here, by what right are you prowling about my premises? Where's your search warrant?' Opening his overcoat, Minton tugged out a handkerchief, mopped his face and then scowled.

'Your head clerk, Mr. Barridge, was murdered today, Mr. Minton. About half-past one. In fact the information has already got into the evening papers.'

'He was — ? I haven't seen the papers yet.' All the aggressiveness seemed to go out of Minton for a moment. His beefy face went a shade redder. 'Barridge was *murdered*? Where? Here?'

'In your office,' Henshaw replied, and motioned to a chair.

'In my office? That's impossible! He didn't have a key.'

'That's as maybe, but there he was. I'm hoping you will be able to tell me something, and of course establish an alibi for yourself. You won't mind telling me where you've been today, of course?'

'But I *do* mind! You're not dealing with an ordinary person, superintendent. I'm a solicitor, remember, and I know the law as well — and maybe better — than you do.'

'Perhaps, sir, I had better make things plainer,' Henshaw said, ignoring the outburst. 'Mr. Barridge was found in your office and as far as I can discover you are the only person with a key to it. He was murdered when the rest of the staff was at lunch and, possibly, the janitor also . . . I surely don't have to remind you, a legal man, that setting up an alibi is a necessity, so that we can check it?'

'What you mean,' Minton said, without looking at the superintendent, 'is that being the sole possessor of the key things look ugly for me?'

Henshaw did not answer.

'You police are an infernally suspicious lot,' Minton growled. 'And you've started bungling already! I didn't have anything to do with Barridge's death. In fact, I doubt if he was worth murdering anyway. A more harmless, spineless man couldn't exist . . . How was he killed? Tell me that — if you're permitted to.'

'With your paperknife.' Henshaw added such details as he considered relevant. 'I am entitled to ask all the questions I consider necessary as long as I think useful information might be forthcoming. You know the Judge's Rules as well as I do.'

'I didn't murder Barridge and I don't know who did,' Minton snapped. 'That's all I have to say.'

'It isn't enough. By criminal law, if I have a definite suspicion against a person — as I have against you because of the circumstances — I should detain you. If, though, you will add an alibi to your denial of the offence, which alibi I can verify, then everything will be all right. It's entirely up to you.'

Minton gave a grim smile at the legal phraseology. Then he said: 'I went to Liverpool.'

'To see whom, sir?'

The solicitor got to his feet and went over to Sally Higson's desk where Henshaw was seated. 'Look here, superintendent, I owe you an apology for the way I spoke when I first came in here. I was shocked . . . '

'That's quite all right.' Henshaw said quietly. 'But shall we get back to the point — about Liverpool?'

'By all means. I went to Liverpool today on special legal business, and I just cannot reveal the identity of the people I saw. That is, not *now*. If you can give me until tomorrow I'll establish my alibi then.'

'I'm afraid that won't do, Mr. Minton. Without casting aspersions, you must know that every minute before the establishment of an alibi makes the alibi easier to arrange. One of the drawbacks of granting bail lics in the fact that the person concerned has the time to establish an alibi and, sometimes, escape justice . . . ' The superintendent shook his head. 'I'm sorry, but I must have the names of the people you saw, and the times at which you saw them. The business you discussed doesn't concern me in the least. For your own sake you must say where you were, and with whom.'

'I went to see a Mr. Gerald Anstruther. He's a well-known Liverpool solicitor and a great friend of mine. Since the nature of the business doesn't matter to you I will add the times. I got into Liverpool at about half-past twelve, leaving here on the ten-thirty train. I had lunch, saw Mr. Anstruther at two o'clock and left again at — '

'That doesn't matter, sir,' Henshaw interrupted. 'Barridge was murdered at approximately one thirty. What happened after that time isn't of the least interest. At which time — one-thirty — you were having lunch in Liverpool, then?'

'At the Martino Restaurant, though if you expect me to prove it I can't.'

'I hardly expect it. Mr. Anstruther will serve quite well. What is his address?'

'Fourteen Wilmington Street. That's not far from the Old Swan district. That's his office address, by the way. I don't know his private one.'

'And yet he's a great friend of yours?' Henshaw glanced up.

'I should have said a great *business* friend. He doesn't know my private address, nor do I know his. When we meet it is in each other's offices.'

'I see. Thanks, Mr. Minton. I'll check back on that. And there is one other thing. You mentioned when you first came in here that you told only Mr. Barridge where you were going. You didn't tell anybody else?'

'I don't explain my movements to my staff,' Minton retorted. 'Barridge was my head clerk and confidential secretary, and he also knew how to keep his mouth shut. He had known for a fortnight that I was intending to go to Liverpool today, but I forbade him to tell anybody because of the confidential nature of my mission.'

'I understand. Now to something else: what is the usual procedure in this office when somebody brings in a case? Say — at random — a suit for divorce. How is it handled?'

The solicitor frowned. 'Why, I see the

person concerned, of course, and hear what they have to say. Then I suggest whatever may be necessary.'

'And where did Mr. Barridge fit into this scheme of things?'

'Being my head clerk he acted on my instructions once I had decided upon a course of action.'

'In that event you will know of the divorce case of Carr v Carr?'

'I never heard of the name. What has it to do with the murder of Barridge, anyway? What are you getting at?'

Henshaw did not answer. Taking out his cigarette case he held it forth and the solicitor took one. The shiny case slipped out of the superintendent's hand abruptly and dropped to the carpet.

'Nerves, super?' Minton questioned dryly, picking it up and handing it back to him.

Henshaw smiled, took a cigarette, and put the case on the blotter.

'The case of Mrs. Carr was being handled by Mr. Barridge,' he said, 'on the grounds that he invariably handled the preliminaries and you the actual case. I understood it to be quite the regular thing.'

'Who told you that?'

'Mrs. Carr herself, who had been informed of the fact by Mr. Barridge.'

'Ridiculous!' Minton drew hard on his cigarette. 'I'm the head of this business. Certainly Barridge wasn't. If he did that sort of thing it was of his own accord and entirely without my knowledge. I take it you found the file of Carr *v* Carr in his office, then? I'd like to have a look at it.'

'So would I,' Henshaw answered briefly. 'There isn't one. No sign of such a case existing, and even less sign of the early love letters she wrote to her husband and which Barridge said were essential as groundwork for the case against him.'

The solicitor gave a slow, incredulous smile.

'You mean to tell me that Barridge actually said that early love letters — love letters — !' he smiled incredulously, 'were essential to the case? Such damned nonsense! Statements by both sides are all that is necessary, with other relative evidence and good grounds for the action, such as cruelty, desertion, alienation — . But love letters! Absurd! Tell me,' Minton finished, 'what was Mrs. Carr suing for? On what grounds?'

'Desertion, I believe. Her husband went off to Australia and left her high and dry.'

'Then you can take it from me that a case like that would definitely be placed before me first.'

'Thanks for clearing that up,' Henshaw mused. 'There's one thing I'd like you to do, Mr. Minton. Open your safe and desk drawers. I'd like to see if there are any references in either if them to this Carr case.'

'There aren't. However, I've nothing to hide. Come and see for yourself.'

Henshaw got up and followed him into the private office. In a few moments Minton had the safe door open and lifted the contents out on to the desk. Henshaw examined them briefly — legal documents in every case — but there was no sign of anything in connection with Carr.

Minton next unlocked the desk drawers

with a considerable amount of key-jangling and hard breathing, but there was not a single item of interest, and, with a troubled frown, Henshaw had to admit the fact.

'I think this Carr business is some sort of trumped-up story,' Minton declared finally.

'I could think the same, sir, but for seeing Mrs. Carr herself,' Henshaw answered — then he changed the topic. 'The paperknife you used, with which Barridge was murdered. It's with us now, of course, but I'd like to know where you originally got it.'

'I bought it at a sale. I don't pretend to be an expert on knives, but it occurred to me it was a nice piece of *bric-a-brac*. I was told that it is a yataghan, an Afghan sword.'

'Then you were misinformed,' Henshaw replied, smiling. 'I would suggest that it is an ordinary, common-or-garden two-edged knife, well disguised to look to the uninitiated like an antique. The genuine yataghan is a slightly curved saber and the cutting edges, two-sided, only extend for a quarter of its length. On your knife the cutting edges go the whole length of the blade, and the blade is straight. The unusually long hilt crosspiece perhaps gives the impression of value — but actually it is quite an ordinary piece of work.'

Minton shrugged. 'So I was swindled. It was my knife and you say Barridge was murdered with it. Not much I can do about it, is there?'

Henshaw watched as Minton returned the various deeds and relocked his safe. As he did the same with the drawers, the superintendent asked a question:

'What was your honest impression of Mr. Barridge?'

'He was trustworthy and a good worker . . . ' Minton crushed out his cigarette in the ashtray. 'But as a man he was a pain in the neck. I have never known a more spiritless individual! He always rushed to obey the slightest order, no matter how difficult it might have been to execute. He never stood up for his rights, and certainly he never had the courage to ask for a rise. I gave him two

154

during the time he worked for me, and I only did that because of the cost-of-living rise and — if you believe it — to salve my own conscience. He was the perfect example of the hackneyed saying, 'What are you, man or mouse?' He was definitely *mouse*.'

'Yet he must have made an enemy ruthless enough to decide to kill him. Seems queer in so mild a man.'

'He had the kind of mildness which was infuriating,' he said. 'Certainly it infuriated me.'

'I shan't need to detain you any longer, Mr. Minton,' Henshaw said finally. 'I'll check that alibi of yours and let you have your statement to sign later.'

'And what about my business? How am I to carry on with you police in the place?'

'As far as I am concerned, sir, there is nothing to prevent you resuming business as usual tomorrow. My enquiries on these premises have finished. You had better notify your staff, though. I sent Standish, Jimmy, and Miss Higson home and they may think they have an indefinite holiday.'

'I'll soon change their minds,' Minton answered, grinning momentarily. 'Anyway, if you want me you have my home address and my 'phone is Shinley eight o. I'll be glad to know how you get on.'

With a nod he left the office and closed the outer door.

'Better type out what he said in here, Willis, and then he can sign it,' Henshaw said pensively.

'Yes, sir. And it sounds a pretty rocky alibi to me. I just can't believe that he doesn't know his friend's private address in Liverpool.'

'Of course he knows it!' Henshaw laughed shortly. 'All he is trying to do is gain time in which to *arrange* his alibi — an old trick. Hence he only gives the office address of his friend, knowing full well we shan't be able to get him at his office at this time of night. If this friend is as important as he seems to be he ought to be in the telephone directory with his home telephone number. If we fail to get anything out of that we can always get the Liverpool police to act and have a word with him for us. In fact we'll start moving now before Minton has a chance to do anything. Get 'directory enquiry', will you, and see if Gerald Anstruther has a private telephone number.'

Willis nodded and turned to the 'phone, dialled, and after a moment or two repeated, 'Orrell seven four two.'

'Get it,' Henshaw instructed, slipping his cigarette case into a small cellophane envelope. 'I'll talk to him.'

The detective-sergeant obeyed instructions and as he waited for the number to be obtained he asked a question. 'The cigarette-case, sir? Minton's prints?'

'Might as well try,' Henshaw agreed. 'It's a pretty ancient method but I often find it effective. Just to check his prints against the others we've got. The only prints that are not my own will be his since nobody else has handled this case for several months — '

'Yes? Hello?' Willis turned back to the 'phone. 'Could I speak to Mr. Gerald Anstruther please? I — ' His expression changed. 'Oh, he is? At — at tea-time? Eh . . . ? Yes, I understand. When will he be back? Tomorrow night? Very well

157

— thanks. No, there is no message.'

'Away?' Henshaw asked laconically.

'Yes.' Willis put the instrument back on the cradle. 'That was his wife speaking. He went away about teatime today on business and didn't say where he was going. He should be back by teatime tomorrow.'

'Wives of these business types don't seem to know much about the activities of their husbands these days,' Henshaw commented.

'Perhaps Minton knew about Anstruther going away,' Willis remarked, thinking. 'In between times he may have an idea where he can contact him and prime him in readiness to give an alibi when you start enquiring.'

'Quite possible,' Henshaw admitted, 'but I'm inclined to suspect Minton — a man intending to commit murder, even to the extent of arranging a 'going away' alibi for himself at the time of the murder occurring, would certainly make sure of the other details. Minton, apparently, has indulged in a clumsy expedient to save his skin for the moment while he thinks out what to do next. I have the notion that his effort to create an alibi is for some *other* reason, to hide where he *really* went.'

'I agree, sir. Question is: what is he covering up for?'

'I've no idea. There were no clues in the safe or in the drawers of the desk in his office. Probably he keeps most of his private stuff at home, somewhere where he feels entirely safe. We may find out about that in time. Men of his calibre have lots of irons in the fire — and if ever a man thought fast this evening he did. He had to gain time — and such is the law I had to let him get away with it.'

Henshaw glanced at the clock and smothered a yawn.

'There's a limit to what we can cover in one day, Willis,' he said. 'And we've a report to make out for the Chief — I've also to send this cigarette-case of mine to the dactylography department in Crayley. Let's get back to headquarters. We've done all we can here.'

8

Minton's temper was not improved when upon entering the house the first person he saw after the maid was his wife.

'Henry, something rather startling has occurred — I had the superintendent of police here this afternoon, asking after you.'

'I know,' Minton answered curtly. 'I found him and his men crawling about my office like flies round a jam jar. Somebody killed Barridge with my paperknife. I've been put through the third degree by that superintendent. Smart man, though. And I'm pretty sure he thinks I'm responsible for the murder. Nice damned thing!'

'It was quite a shock to me when he turned up this afternoon and said he wanted you. I told him that you were away, and that I didn't know when you would return. I did right, didn't I?'

'That,' Henry Minton answered, 'was

all you *could* tell him — Excuse me, Ethel, will you? I've an important telephone call to make. Tell Susan I want a meal — and quickly.'

He strode out from the room, crossed the hall, and settled himself at the telephone. He asked the operator for 'Manchester — City six-seven-two-one.'

'Stag Hotel?' Minton asked, as he was put through. 'I wish to speak to a Mr. Gerald Anstruther. This is Henry Minton calling, and tell him it's urgent.'

Pause. Then, 'You're through, sir.'

'Hello, there, Henry!' came a bluff, genial voice over the wire. 'What causes you to waste hard-earned money on me? Or is it just friendship?'

'Listen, Gerald, this is important,' Minton said tensely. 'I never needed a friend more than I do at this moment. Have you been at your office in Liverpool today?'

'Yes, of course — until about four-thirty, then I left for Manchester — '

'Ah! I thought my memory hadn't failed me. You told me you were going when we fixed up the Barton case.'

'What if I did?'

'My remembering that fact may save me from disaster,' Minton said. 'I realized that you would be in Liverpool today and going to Manchester tonight, staying at the Stag Hotel, and I also realized that you wouldn't be telling anybody where you were going because of the nature of your business . . . That may help me a lot. I'm in one devil of a spot . . . Look, Gerald, I want to use you for an alibi.'

'Alibi?' Anstruther sounded suspicious. 'What have you done, man?'

'Actually nothing, but it's not easy to convince the police of that fact. In time they will inevitably get in touch with you and ask if I was with you today. I'm relying on you to say 'yes'. I know,' Minton added, with a heavy laugh, 'that it's a pretty tall order, but we're old friends. We understand each other.'

'Yes, of course we do, but — is it a woman or something? Your wife on the warpath? Can't you tell me what's happened?'

'I would if I could see you personally. It's risky over the 'phone.'

'Well, since it isn't a woman I'll make one guess. It's that head clerk of yours — Barridge. He was murdered today, wasn't he? I read it in the evening paper.'

Minton looked bitterly in front of him. Henshaw had mentioned that news had leaked into it.

In point of fact, the janitor had been responsible for that. Local newshounds, always watching the movements of the police in quest of something sensational, had very soon got the facts out of Baxter and transferred them, suitably played down until full police permission was obtained, to the local paper. The news-agencies had done the rest and carried the bare details in their later editions.

'There isn't much information in it yet,' Anstruther resumed, 'but it does say that your head clerk was found dead in the office of Henry Minton, solicitor, of Hadlam.'

'Damn those reporters,' Minton growled.

'We are good friends, Henry,' Anstruthrer said, 'but I don't feel like involving myself in anything connected with murder. That's dynamite! I wouldn't mind helping you out on some trivial matter, such as spending an evening with a lady of your fancy, but not when it comes to murder. Too risky, and I've my reputation to think of. Sorry, old man. Ask me something easier next time and I'll be glad to oblige.'

The line clicked and Minton slowly realized that Gerald Anstruther had not been quite the unswerving friend he had imagined. Blast the newspapers! Minton started at a tap on the door and his wife came in.

'If you're ready for your meal, Henry, it's waiting for you,' she announced quietly.

'Oh, yes — I'll come . . . Look here, Ethel . . . Did you gather the impression from the superintendent that he suspects I murdered Barridge?'

'I just didn't gather anything of what he was thinking. But it goes without saying that you didn't murder Barridge — doesn't it?'

* * *

The Chief Constable for the county, Colonel Wilton, was waiting when Henshaw and the detective-sergeant returned to the police station.

'Good evening, sir,' Henshaw greeted him formally.

Colonel Wilton was a long, bony man with ginger hair at the back of his head and none at the front. Small grey eyes peered shrewdly from either side of an overthick nose and a tight mouth and chunk of a chin made him appear uncommonly resourceful.

'I thought I'd see how you're getting on,' he explained, as Henshaw settled at the desk and Willis in a chair by the door. 'I've been expecting to hear from you since you 'phoned this afternoon and said you'd been called to a murder at Minton's office. How far have you got?'

'I was going to send in my report — '

'Of course, but now I'm here I want the facts. Let me have the details to date.'

So Henshaw gave them, trying to disguise something of the weariness he felt. The Colonel sat back in his chair and did not once interrupt.

'So that's the way it is,' he said at

length. 'Three possible suspects — Mrs. Carr, Henry Minton, and maybe even this chap Standish, since he doesn't seem able to prove his alibi. Not unexpected, though, in a crowded café.'

'Just what I think, sir. In his case, however, there doesn't seem to be any motive. On the other hand, Mrs. Carr fits the bill because her height and Barridge's make the stabbing-line of the knife seem possible. Against that I am puzzled as to how she got Barridge into Minton's office. No key has turned up — no second key, that is. Nor do I think she would return to the lion's den so calmly if she had committed the murder. That the criminal returns to the scene of the crime is, of course, so much nonsense . . . As to Minton . . . Well, as I say, I think he would have taken every precaution regarding his alibi.'

'I'm inclined to agree with you,' the Chief Constable said, after a pause. 'How about suicide? Have you considered that possibility?'

'I've given it some thought,' Henshaw admitted, 'only at present I don't quite see how a man could stab himself under the left scapula and get the knife in a straight line. It would go *upwards*. I've tried it in pantomime. It would demand a contortionist to get that straight-line drive. And even if I were to give suicide serious thought I can't see what motive Barridge would have for it.'

'There might have been the very obvious reason that he was weary of life. He was, from all accounts, pretty much at the mercy of everybody else. And don't forget that disease of his — endocarditis. Since he had that — '

'But why should he want to commit suicide because of that, sir? He was likely to die anyway because of it, though whether he knew that or not I don't know yet. But I'll find out. As far as I can see, suicide would not have been an advantage to him. Add to that that he chose Minton's office and used a paperknife, and the thing becomes fantastic. No — ' The superintendent shook his head. 'At the moment, I'm afraid I still incline to murder. It's puzzling though: three suspects and all of them having a factor in their favour that suggests they didn't do it.'

'What will your next move be?'

'For one thing I've got to check Minton's alibi the moment I can get in touch with Gerald Anstruther, which won't be until tomorrow evening, I'm afraid. Then I have to see Mrs. Barridge and see what I can discover about Barridge's life and habits, to find out if he had possible enemies, and so forth. I have also to trace where the woman's brooch and hairgrip came from ... I'll dig something out before long, sir, never fear. We have quite a few things to go on, but at present they are unrelated. It's a matter of finding out which part belongs to which.'

The Colonel got to his feet with a smile. 'I'll leave it to you, Henshaw: I've complete faith in your ability. Let me know how you get on, and send in your report. From a study of it I may have a new angle to suggest.'

Henshaw saw his superior to the door — then he returned to his desk. He studied the photograph of the office in which Barridge had died — which photographs had come during the evening — and the complete report from the dactylography department in Crayley attached to the double-bladed knife with which the murder had been committed. The report said:

> *Fingerprint Report (re William Barridge deceased): Prints on knife hilt are of the twinned-loop, nine-ridge variety and are repeated throughout the office in question. No other prints are distinguishable on the knife. They are not those of the dead man and therefore are presumed to be those of Henry Minton.*

Henshaw felt in his pocket and pulled out his cigarette case in the protective envelope. He pressed the button on his desk and the sergeant-in-charge came in. Henshaw scribbled a note:

> *Check fingerprints on this cigarette case by the copy. Fingerprints you have on file believed to be those of Henry Minton. If the prints on this*

case tally then the prints on the knife — and other objects — are Henry Minton's.

Henshaw(Sup't.)

Sealing the note up inside the envelope he handed it to the sergeant. 'Tell Parker, or whoever is on duty, to take this over to Crayley right away,' he instructed. 'And to get a reply before coming back. I'll wait.'

'Even if we prove the prints on the knife *are* Minton's, sir, it doesn't get us much further,' Willis pointed out, as the sergeant left. 'He must have handled that knife dozens of times when opening his correspondence.'

'True, but we don't know that they are *his* prints. The experts merely assume so, which is all they can do until they have comparison prints which we know belong to Minton. There is also something else which occurs to me,' Henshaw looked again at the photographs of the disordered office. 'Before the murder occurred there was a struggle. That fact may be very useful to us.'

'How so, sir?'

'If you were fighting for your life, Willis, you'd hit out at your attacker, wouldn't you? Even if you were a weak-kneed specimen such as Barridge? Nobody, however retiring, dies without making a mighty fight to survive.'

'Well, yes — if he had the opportunity.'

'He did — the signs of struggle make it self-evident. I'm thinking that there ought to be some interesting revelations under his fingernails. There is no better place to find traces of the attacker's clothes — or even blood, though from the look of Minton he hasn't any scratches or marks.'

Henshaw drew the telephone to him. In a few moments he had contacted the superintendent of the Crayley forensic department. 'I want you to send some-body down to the mortuary, Bob, and get some samples of the dirt from under Barridge's fingernails. Let me know what the micro-analysts have to say when they've finished. Pardon? Yes, the body's there. First thing in the morning will be soon enough for the report . . . Huh? No, I'm not much nearer yet, but I will be with the help of experts. 'Bye for now.'

Henshaw rang off. 'We'll see what we get out of that,' he commented, meeting Willis's glance. 'If Minton didn't change his suit during the day — which I consider most unlikely — we might find microscopic traces of it under Barridge's nails — if Minton was the murderer.'

'Or fur if it was Mrs. Carr,' Willis added.

'Uh-huh.' Henshaw found the envelope containing Barridge's belongings and tipped them out on the desk.

'This bent hairgrip still puzzles me. I don't think it belonged to the janitor's wife . . . Not that I'm going to rack my brains over it tonight,' he added, putting the effects back into a locker. 'I'll just wait until that report comes back from the fingerprint department and then I'm going to call it a day. You can skip if you want.'

'Thank you, sir. See you in the morning.'

Henshaw settled in his chair to wait. An hour later the fingerprint report came back:

Fingerprints are definitely those of Henry Minton.

9

Following the news of her husband's mysterious murder, and her identification of the body at the mortuary, Mrs. Emily Barridge existed in something of a daze. It was not the confusion of deep-seated grief. It was a turbulence of mind created by the knowledge that she had completely to reorganize her life.

It took her all the Monday afternoon to decide what to tell the children when they came home from school — and, sensibly, she finally decided to tell them the truth. The only thing she suppressed was the word 'murder' and said instead that their father had been 'killed'.

This revelation produced little grief. The three children were momentarily quiet, wondered why they were forbidden to leave the house — for Mrs. Barridge had no wish for them to become involved in neighbourly gossip. Besides, the superintendent might call and make enquiries:

and surely he would wish to question the children?

It was evening before Mrs. Barridge's slow working brain brought her to a decision. First she must discover how much insurance she could claim, and then decide where extra money was to come from. The fact that she might have to turn out and work in order to keep things going secretly appalled her — at first — then she thought more kindly of it as it opened up the prospect of social contact, change from her grinding routine. Perhaps in time she might even find a man — or a sucker — willing enough to take on herself and three noisy children.

After tea she made the three children settle to their homework, whilst she brought the insurance policy from the sideboard and sat down to study it. She couldn't unravel it, so in the end she wrote a postcard to the local representative of the World Insurance Trust and asked him to call.

Then — Lucy having been dispatched to post the card — Mrs. Barridge sat thinking upon the possibilities of a boarder in the house. The room her husband had used as his 'den' could be turned out — the junk thrown in the dustbin — and a 'paying guest' lured in. Tomorrow, Emily Barridge decided, she would get busy and turn the room out. Or the day after — at any rate, not before she *had* to.

Discovering with supreme disgust that her husband had not been provident enough to leave a will, even though she could have sworn he had mentioned it some time or other that he had made one — she went to bed and packed the children off too, an hour and a half early.

Next morning, Mrs. Barridge kept the children at home for two reasons — one, because the morning paper showed that the murder had leaked into the daily Press and therefore might produce endless repercussions of scandal at school; and two, because she needed all three children to do a lot of hard work tidying up the 'den'. She just did not feel up to doing it herself . . . Furthest from her mind seemed to be mystification as to her husband's murderer. Her chief concern was her own plight because of it.

Her first visitor after breakfast was a short, thin man in a tight-fitting overcoat and exceptionally smart bowler hat. Lucy opened the door to him and he was shown into the front drawing room where, briefcase on his knees, he waited for Mrs. Barridge to come lumbering in. At her arrival he jumped up with dynamic energy and gripped her hand.

'Douglas Casper, madam,' he explained, handing over his card. 'Of World Insurance Trust. I received your card and came right away. Meantime, may I extend my own and the company's condolences in your sad loss?' The agent's voice sank a semitone lower and then faded right out.

'Thanks,' Mrs. Barridge responded. 'Won't you sit down, Mr. Casper? If you'll wait a moment I'll get the policy.'

After a moment or two Mrs. Barridge came back with the policy. Casper took it and sat poring over its closely-printed complexity.

'Hmmm,' he said at last, 'paid up to date, taken out four years ago. And an additional clause added two weeks ago which slightly altered the amount of premium payable.'

Emily Barridge, seated at the table and breathing heavily, gave a start.

'Additional clause?' she repeated. '*What* additional clause?'

'This one here, madam — section nine, sub-section six. Namely that the policy is rendered void in the event of the suicide of the holder.'

'But . . . ' Mrs. Barridge wrestled with unaccustomed difficulties. 'Aren't *all* policies void where there is suicide on the part of the holder?'

'No.' Douglas Casper was quite sure of the fact. 'Only when a definite clause is inserted, like this one here.'

'But when did my husband make that stipulation? I know that he took out the original policy four years ago because I made him do it, so the children and I could have something if anything ever happened to him. I don't remember him saying anything about a suicide clause. Two weeks ago?' Mrs. Barridge shook her head. 'No, he never mentioned it.'

'Then I imagine it must have slipped

his memory, madam. As a matter of fact I had quite a long talk with him, and in the end I saw to it that the necessary adjustment was made. He sent for me, you see — to call at his office. Or rather the office of Mr. Minton.'

'I wonder why he had the clause inserted?' Emily Barridge looked absently at the cabinet gramophone in the corner and frowned. 'And for the life of me I can't think why he didn't tell me.'

'Quite,' Casper admitted, shrugging, then after another tight-nostril survey of the policy he added: 'In any case the suicide clause does not enter into it since your husband was murdered — that is according to present police reports. The moment that fact is definitely established by the court the company will pay, naturally.'

'Definitely established? Then that means I have to wait?'

'I'm afraid so, Mrs. Barridge. We have to have the facts first, of course. Assumption of murder is hardly enough guarantee for an insurance company. We need legal proof that your husband died through any other cause *but* suicide.'

'I see,' Emily Barridge said, though she looked completely bewildered.

'You may rest assured that I shall be watching out for your interests.' Casper got up briskly. 'You just hang on to that policy until the matter of your husband's death is entirely cleared up — then I'll be here and I'm sure it will be with your cheque. Good day.'

After Casper departed, Mrs. Barridge vented her annoyance on the three children and set them the task of cleaning out the 'den'. Actually it was a small boxroom at the top of the stairs, and in it her husband had been wont to do a good deal of his legal 'homework' away from the endless distractions and arguments of the household.

'I haven't the heart to be turning over your poor father's things up there,' Mrs. Barridge said, sitting down at the uncleared breakfast table to do a further spell of thinking. 'I still can't believe that we shall never see him again — that he'll never bring up my tea in the morning any more. I don't think I'm ever going to get over the shock. Just tidy the room up, dears,' she finished, 'and if you find anything you don't know what to do with just tell me.'

Thus instructed the three children clattered upstairs to commence operations, and for ten minutes or so Mrs. Barridge heard them bumping and banging — then Lucy came racing downstairs, covered in dust and her hair disordered, carrying in one hand what appeared to be a bundle of old letters.

'Do I throw these in the fire or the dustbin, mummy?' she asked.

Her mother took them. There were two bundles — or rather one fairly thick bundle and then three letters, both lots tied in pink lawyer's tape.

'Oh, these letters will be from your Uncle James, love,' she said. 'Out in Australia. And these'll be . . . '

Emily Barridge's eyes sharpened. Now she came to notice it the packet of three letters had no envelopes: there were just the letters themselves. The opening words — *Dearest Snookums* — and the closing line, *Your loving Jenny* — made her stare hard and then gasp a little to herself.

'And there's these Australian newspapers, and these,' Lucy added. From inside the top of her gymslip she dragged out a batch of overseas newspapers and several betting cards, dumping them on the table. Mrs. Barridge stared at the latter blankly. The thought of betting cards connected with her husband was something she just could not reconcile. What was even more astonishing, several of the horses named on the betting cards had been ticked off in red ink.

Puzzled by the long silence, Lucy again asked plaintively what she was to do.

'You'd better — Go and see who that is,' her mother ordered, as the front door bell rang.

Lucy went, and found herself looking in awe at the uniformed figures of Superintendent Henshaw and Detective-sergeant Willis.

'Your mother in, love?' Henshaw enquired pleasantly, and too utterly overwhelmed to speak, Lucy shyly motioned them inside, and into the kitchen.

'Good morning, Mrs. Barridge.' Henshaw

took off his uniform-cap and shook hands. 'I'm Superintendent Henshaw: this is Detective-sergeant Willis. I trust you are sufficiently recovered from the shock of your husband's death to answer a few questions?'

'Yes, I think so.' Mrs. Barridge motioned to two bentwood chairs and then sat down again herself. 'Be off with you, Lucy,' she added. 'I'll call if I need you.'

The child nodded and scampered from the room.

'Now, madam, at the risk of this interview being painful to you, I'd like to ask you one or two questions about your late husband.'

'Of course,' Emily Barridge agreed, looking appropriately sombre.

'Can you call to mind any enemies your husband might have had? Take your time to think about it. There may have been some occasion when your husband mentioned the fact.'

Mrs. Barridge laughed shortly. 'I just don't have to think about that, superintendent. He was so meek and mild he just couldn't have had any. He was always that way. Mind you, I had hopes, when we were first married, that he would become bolder as the years advanced — but he didn't.'

'I see. In this case he perhaps had more friends than enemies?'

Before she could answer there came a series of stunning concussions from somewhere upstairs. Presumably the children were doing their work thoroughly.

'I'd say he didn't have either,' she said at last. 'He was too reserved to make either friends *or* enemies.'

'Can you remember if your husband had anything particularly significant to say yesterday before he started off for the office?'

'No . . . Of course, we had our usual arguments . . . '

'Arguments? About what?'

'Chiefly about him being so slow. I used to keep telling him to stand up for himself more than he did. Stuck in that solicitor's office all his life! Never getting any further than just being a head clerk! We had no end of rows about it.'

Further bumps and thuds from above

and, afar off, the squeal of Lucy and an enigmatic reference to ' . . . awful *beast!*'

'My husband said he couldn't get on,' Emily Barridge said moodily. 'He used to say he couldn't change his nature. Been reserved ever since he was a boy. Didn't mind being picked on because he'd *always* been picked on. Then at other times he used to say that it was his health that made him quiet, and willing to be trodden on. Funny thing, though, for all his quietness he never forgot an insult, or when anybody slighted him. Even yesterday morning, just before he left for the office, he was saying that as a young man girls used to take advantage of him, and then laugh in his face. After all these years he was still very bitter about it.'

'Was his health bad?' Henshaw enquired.

'Good heavens, no! In all the time we were married he was only ill once — not very long ago. He got a severe attack of rheumatism, only just missing rheumatic fever, according to Dr. Blandish. But he soon got over it — '

'Just rheumatism? Nothing else?'

'Not as far as I know. Outside of that

attack I never knew him to be ill. He thought too much about his health, if you ask me. Always saying he'd die suddenly when it came. Come to think of it, he was right there!'

Henshaw was silent for a moment, absently considering the disorder of the kitchen. 'You cannot tell me of anything unusual about your husband?' he asked finally. 'Any peculiar characteristic?'

'Only one thing. He had the keenest nose of anybody I've ever known. Smell things a mile off, he could, where I'd never notice 'em — or the children either.'

'Mmm — unusual,' Henshaw admitted; then, 'Did he ever discuss his business at home?'

'Not much. He knew I wasn't interested in his dry old legal stuff; and what went on in his office was private, I suppose. He used to do a lot of legal work at home here, though. He had a little room at the top of the stairs. As you can hear, the kids are cleaning it out now.'

Henshaw's eyes wandered to the papers and letters on the table, together with the betting cards. From these his gaze strayed to Willis who was inconspicuously making notes in shorthand.

'Before your husband left yesterday did he mention that he was sending something to a James Barridge of Melbourne Australia? By registered mail?'

'No. But it isn't unusual. He fairly fawned over that brother of his — he was a regular idol to my husband.' Emily Barridge stopped and looked wondering. 'Why, *did* my husband send something to Australia?'

'He sent either a letter or a parcel yesterday morning,' Henshaw answered.

'Then I can't think what it could have been.'

'Was there any particular reason why your husband admired his brother so much?'

'Because he is successful,' Mrs. Barridge answered. 'He went out to Australia as a young man — always keeping in touch with my husband through the post — and has made quite a pile of money and a reputation for himself as a big consulting engineer. William wrote to him constantly, and even kept all the letters he got back. That will give you an idea of their devotion to each other. In fact — ' Mrs. Barridge turned to the table — 'here are some of the letters my daughter just brought down from the room he used to use.'

Henshaw glanced at the envelopes and nodded slowly. 'I'd rather like to retain these, Mrs. Barridge, if I may? Every sidelight on your husband is useful to us in endeavoring to trace his murderer.'

'Take them by all means,' she agreed.

Henshaw had to think fast not to appear startled. The handing over of the Australian letters had revealed the other three letters that had been underneath. The sight of the name 'Jenny' was enough to set a whole chain of thoughts moving. He managed to appear undisturbed and put the Australian letters in his pocket. Then from the same pocket he brought to view the brooch that had been in Barridge's belongings.

'I wonder, Mrs. Barridge, does this happen to be yours?' he asked.

She took it, and as she examined it, her

fleshy face scowled.

'No, it isn't mine, and I never saw it before!' Her voice hardened as she handed it back. 'I never had any jewelry as nice as that, or as expensive.'

'It is possible, madam, that your husband might have picked it up in the street, don't forget. We can't jump to conclusions — '

'Perhaps you can't, as an official, but I can. I just never could *believe* that a man could really be so quiet as William. It made me think sometimes that maybe he got up to some monkey tricks when he was away from home. He used to say that he wasn't interested in gambling, or anything like that — but he took good care to read up about the horses. Only yesterday morning he was reading about them when I was getting breakfast. Not much point in reading about the horses when you don't bet, is there?'

'Was it a habit of his to do that?' Henshaw asked.

'Well, no — I only remember him doing it for about the last two or three weeks or so. Then there are these!' Mrs.

Barridge made a dive at the pile on the table. 'My kids dug them out of the room this morning. Look for yourself, superintendent! Betting cards! Horses ticked off!'

The betting cards were dated for the previous year and carried the name of 'Sporting Bob King', one of Hadlam's most prominent bookmakers.

'Interesting,' Henshaw commented.

'So I think if he'd back horses on the sly — and it looks as if he did — he might quite easily have had some woman in tow somewhere. Wouldn't surprise me a bit! He as good as told me I got on his nerves, and he certainly got on mine.'

'Did your husband make a will?' Henshaw asked.

'I'm convinced that he said he did — but I can't find it.'

'And was he insured?'

'The insurance man had only just gone when you came. Yes, he was insured. Took it out four years ago. Only there is something I don't quite understand. A fortnight ago he had a clause added to the policy — that it should not be payable in the event of suicide. Why do you imagine he did that?'

Henshaw shrugged. 'Sorry, I'm afraid I don't know what went on in your husband's mind. A fortnight ago, eh? Until then, had he died from any cause whatever — including murder or suicide — the insurance would have been payable?'

'So the agent said. I can't imagine why he had to put that clause in — unless it was to lower the premium payment, which it did. Anyway, he wasn't the sort of man to have the nerve to take his own life. I said to him yesterday that I was getting so sick of things I felt like putting an end to it all, and he said I hadn't got the courage — that it takes a lot of it to commit suicide.'

'He said that; did he? Not very flattering to you, was it?'

The woman's eyes brightened suddenly. 'I believe I *have* it! Knowing he never *would* commit suicide, and evidently knowing through being in the legal business that he could lower his payments by having that clause inserted, he decided to do it. That must have been it.'

'Possibly,' Henshaw agreed. 'You said that you believe your husband had a 'woman in tow.' I don't believe that you base your assumption so much on his apparent interest in horses, or the brooch, as on that letter there from 'Jenny'.'

Emily Barridge looked down sharply at the letters on the table, the three of them tied in pink tape, and the name of 'Jenny' clearly visible.

'All right,' she answered, shrugging, 'why should I deny it? What would *you* think if suddenly you found these in a drawer? I was just reading this top one when you arrived. It's certainly nothing *I* ever sent him — and besides my name isn't Jenny . . . I begin to think that my husband was two-faced after all! Pretending to be so meek and mild and all the time he was probably worse than the worst of them!'

'Would you mind if I saw those letters?' Henshaw asked, and with a gesture of disgust the woman handed them to him.

'By all means! He's dead now, so what do I care what sort of things he did? I know what *I* think . . . 'Dear Snookums' indeed!'

The ghost of a smile crossed Willis's face, but not Henshaw's. In a few minutes he covered all three letters and saw enough in that time to convince him that they were worth careful attention in the privacy of headquarters.

'These, and the letters from your brother-in-law, may be invaluable to me, Mrs. Barridge,' he said finally. 'I'd like your permission to retain them for a while, along with the rest of your husband's effects.'

'As you like,' she answered moodily — then at a particularly violent bump from upstairs she frowned impatiently. A voice yelled from the top of the stairs.

'Mummy! *Mummy!* What do we do with Dad's *Home Doctor*? Does it go in the front-room bookcase with the others?'

'It's too big for there!' objected a boy's voice.

'Excuse me a moment,' Mrs. Barridge apologized, getting up. 'I'll have to settle this — '

'I'd rather like to see the room where your husband worked,' Henshaw said, rising also.

'All right. Come on up.'

Henshaw motioned Willis to stay where he was, and then followed the woman's ponderous bulk up the staircase and into the room Barridge had used. Under the efforts of three extremely dirty children, it had become a glorious confusion of boxes, papers, and shifted furniture. 'I'm clearing it out for a boarder,' she added, by way of explanation.

'Have to do something now William's gone, that is until I get the insurance money. And I hope you won't be too long in dealing with this business, superintendent. I could do with that money.'

'You can rest assured, Mrs. Barridge, that I shall work as rapidly as possible,' Henshaw answered.

'My husband's *death*,' Mrs. Barridge added, emphasizing the word, 'has made a terrible difference to us.'

Henshaw interpreted her look that, as yet, the children were not conversant with all the facts. He nodded to her quietly and then turned to take in the details of the room.

Amongst the jumble was a bentwood

chair, a small writing-desk with a slanting top, and a chest of drawers with all its drawers half tugged out and the various contents either on the floor or the top of the writing-desk.

'Where did you find those letters and cards, youngster?' he asked the girl, as she struggled, with her younger brother, to pull the writing-desk out of the corner.

'In the chest of drawers, sir.'

'Was the drawer where you found them locked?'

Since the child coloured and looked shamefaced the elder brother answered for her, with a petulant out-thrusting of the lips.

'Yes, it *was* locked — but since nobody would have the key except my Dad, and that key would be with the police — '

'Police!' his mother echoed. 'How do you know about the police?'

The boy shrugged. 'Dad was murdered, wasn't he? I'm old enough to read the papers, you know. Anyway, I decided we should smash the drawer open with a screwdriver. That was the only drawer we found locked. Nothing else in it except those letters, betting cards, and the Melbourne newspapers.'

'Melbourne newspapers?' Henshaw repeated.

'Those were they on the table down-stairs,' Mrs. Barridge explained. 'James used to send them regularly.'

'I noticed the newspapers,' Henshaw answered, 'but I thought they were old British ones.'

He dropped the subject for a moment and waded through the lumber and rubbish on the floor to a massive volume on top of the chest of drawers.

'That's the *Home Doctor*,' Lucy said. 'I wanted you to tell me what to do with it, mummy.'

Henshaw picked the volume up and glanced through it briefly; then he set it down again. It was a remarkably compre-hensive work and apart from the subject matter was filled with all manner of shiny plates depicting those curiously revolting pictures of sausage-like entrails.

'Was your husband interested in this kind of thing, Mrs. Barridge?' he enquired.

'He may have been.' The woman shrugged indifferently. 'He was always finicky about his health, as I told you. The only reason that book's here is because it's too tall to fit on the shelf with his legal books in the case downstairs. There are dozens of those — all useless junk they'll be now, too,' she added reflectively.

'I see . . . ' Henshaw turned his attention to all the drawers and cupboards he could find, but amidst the piles of stuff he found nothing to interest him.

'I'm in the way up here,' he said, smiling, 'and I think I've asked all I need — so for the time being, Mrs. Barridge, I had better be getting along. Have you any particular use for those Australian newspapers downstairs?'

'Make good firelighters,' she said.

'I'd rather like them myself, to read, if I may. I'm very interested in Australia. May even emigrate there some day — '

'Oh, then take the lot!' the woman exclaimed.

'That's very kind of you. I'll pick them up as I go out — No, don't bother to come down. I'll send along a typewritten statement of what you have told me before long, and you can sign it . . . For the court proceedings later, of course.'

Emily Barridge nodded, and with a last vision of her surrounded by the disorder of the room and her three children in the background, Henshaw returned downstairs. He scooped up the bundle of newspapers from the table, jerked his head to Willis, and they left the house together.

*　*　*

'Well, sir,' Willis said, as they reached the car, 'we have at least tracked down the three letters of Jennifer Carr. 'Jenny' means Jennifer, of course.'

'Of course,' Henshaw agreed, tossing the Australian newspapers into the back of the car.

'Why the papers, sir?'

Henshaw shrugged. 'You can never know too much about the people involved in a problem, and since the newspapers belonged to Barridge I might as well look through them . . . Not to the station just yet,' he added, as the detective-sergeant switched on the ignition. 'I want a word with Dr. Blandish. That was the name of the doctor who treated Barridge for his rheumatism. Might see if he can give us anything on the endocarditis angle. Drive to the Medical Centre and make enquiry as to his address.'

'Right, sir.'

Within five minutes Willis had established the doctor's address, and ten minutes later they had driven to it. The doctor had just come in from his morning rounds and, though busy, agreed to see the two officials of the law.

'Good morning, doctor,' Henshaw said. 'I won't take up much of your valuable time, but there's a matter in which you can help me. It concerns William Barridge.'

The doctor was a tall, black-haired, saturnine man who looked as though he rarely smiled. 'Somehow I expected it would,' he said. 'I read of the case in the morning paper, and noticed that you are in charge of it. How can I help you?'

'You were Mr. Barridge's usual doctor.

I understand,' Henshaw said, 'that he contracted rheumatism recently, and you attended him?'

'Oh, yes, indeed! About a year ago. It was a short and severe attack while it lasted. I think he got it through sitting on damp grass.'

'I see. Tell me one thing: did you know that he contracted endocarditis?'

The doctor tightened his lips for a moment and then nodded slowly.

'I did, yes. It was a direct outcome of his rheumatic attack. He came to me for advice when he was getting over the actual rheumatism, mentioned a feeling of discomfort about the heart, and demanded to know the truth. I told him that he had endocarditis, but that if taken in time the trouble could probably be greatly alleviated, if not cured entirely. I don't know whether the facts frightened him or not, but I *do* know that he never came to see me again.'

'Naturally, only he knew of this ailment outside yourself?'

'Yes.' The doctor gave a dry smile. 'That is except for whoever told you.'

'My informant was the divisional-surgeon, so you've nothing to worry over. All right, doctor, thanks. That's all I wanted to know.'

Again the two men took their departure and returned to the car.

'Back to headquarters,' Henshaw said. 'I want to take a good look at those letters from Jennifer Carr.'

Willis had been driving for a few minutes towards the town centre when he said: 'Since Barridge contracted endocarditis, a fatal heart trouble, *after* taking out his life insurance, it was still valid. What I can't understand is why he had that clause added about suicide — unless he did it purely to cut down the premium expense, as Mrs. Barridge thinks. It's peculiar, though, that he happened to do it a fortnight ago, since at that time — so we're told — he first met Jennifer Carr.'

'Exactly,' Henshaw agreed. 'And I'm beginning to think the two factors are not so coincidental, either.'

10

On his return to the police station Henshaw wasted no time in settling down to study his various 'prizes,' Willis sitting beside him at the desk. The first thing they tackled were the letters signed 'Jenny'.

They were short letters, perhaps no more than 250 words, penned apparently in a woman's hand, and each one headed with a day instead of a date, respectively 'Wednesday, 'Thursday', and 'Friday.'

'This way of dating a letter gets me down!' Henshaw exclaimed impatiently. 'Why on earth can't people put the *date*? The day can mean any month, any year, any time.'

Willis nodded but said nothing.

'And makes some letters — of this type especially — doubly dangerous,' Henshaw went on, musing. 'Each letter is addressed to 'Dear Snookums' — , which, putting aside the idiotic aspect for a moment, can mean anybody. There's no getting away from 'Jenny', though: that's plain enough. No envelopes. And — most important point — the address has been cut off the top of the notepaper. The edge has been guillotined with a sharp blade.'

'Yes, looks like it,' the detective-sergeant agreed, examining the notepaper closely. 'The experts will soon verify it anyway. I never read letters with such endearment,' he added, grinning a little. 'Obviously Jenny must have been deeply in love when she wrote them.'

'No doubt; but do you believe that she was ever enough in love with Barridge to write them to him, calling him 'Snookums'?'

'Since they were found in a locked drawer in his private room I'd say 'Yes', but because she seemed, quite frankly, to repulse all his efforts at making advances I'd say 'No'. On the one hand they might be letters two years old and well preserved, sent to her husband — as she told us — and then handed to Barridge as a basis for divorce action. On the other hand she might be a liar and the letters might only be a fortnight old and addressed exclusively to Barridge for whom she really had a passion.'

'Which I find hard to believe! Anyway,' Henshaw added, 'it can easily be settled. Fortunately this is blue-black ink, iron tannin. There's nothing like it when a tintometer gets to work. It will tell us infallibly how old these letters really are. What I shall do is confront Mrs. Carr with these letters and see what reaction I get, then afterwards — whatever her answer — I'll hand them over to the experts for examination. At the same time I'll tackle Mrs. Carr about the brooch.'

Henshaw put the letters carefully in his wallet and picked up the bundle that had been sent by James Barridge from Australia. In silence he and Willis began to read through them.

In no particular had they anything to distinguish them from quite normal letters of brother to brother. Throughout them, interpolated amidst details of his Australian activities, there gleamed something of the vigour and enterprise of James Barridge, obviously a man of exceptionally generous disposition and constantly trying to urge his reticent brother to make a struggle and climb the heights.

'No wonder he admired his brother so much,' Willis remarked presently.

'Mmmm,' Henshaw said absently. 'Listen to this bit — *If at any time you want anything sent from Australia, just let me know. I know things are pretty tight with you. Or, if ever you want to plan a surprise for somebody — say for a birthday or something — why not send me the present and tell me by letter where you wish it sent to in England? Just put in a label and I'll mail it off gladly, unopened. Nothing like a surprise, Billy, from six thousand miles away! Don't forget, now. Only too glad: any time.*'

'That,' the detective-sergeant said, 'seems to make for a bit of light in the darkness at last! Suppose that that registered package Barridge sent was all part of a surprise to be sent back here to England?'

'Right!' Henshaw exclaimed. '*If* it was a parcel, and from the sealing-wax and string I'm inclined to think it was. Let's assume for a moment that it was a parcel. It was sent to James Barridge: that we know. It would take about six weeks to reach Australia, and if sent right back from there it wouldn't be here before another six weeks. All told — '

Henshaw reached forward and examined the calendar. 'All told it could not get here much before the end of April. Since James Barridge said he would gladly send anything unopened if he got a label and instructions it means a letter must have gone separately, maybe by airmail. It's all guesswork, of course, but it does seem to hang together.'

On the calendar memo. for the last week in April he wrote, *Parcel from Australia?*

'I can instruct the post-office to be on the lookout for a parcel addressed from Australia to either Mrs. Barridge, Mrs. Carr, or Mr. Minton, the only three likely people with whom William Barridge had any real connection. It won't be addressed to anybody likely to arouse the suspicions of Brother James. We've also found out that William B. had very few friends in Hadlam to whom he'd be likely to send parcels. It's all we can do — but if we do find out the name of the addressee we can ask that person to open the parcel in our presence . . .

'Of course,' Henshaw went on, 'if it was simply something William B. sent to his brother we shall therefore hear no more about it. What I will do is have the Melbourne police make enquiries and see what James Barridge has to say for himself. That may clear the air a lot.'

Henshaw resumed his study of the letters from Down Under. He found little else of interest. The references seemed to be of a purely personal nature — then Willis found something and handed the letter across.

Henshaw read:

. . . and I am sure you will find the Melbourne Herald *instructive. I shall be sending it to you every week. It will give you interesting sidelights on Australia generally. If you, Emily, and the children ever think of emigrating*

you will have a good idea of what awaits you. Why don't you seriously consider the project? Much more exciting than being stuck in that lawyer's office, and I'll be here at your back. Wake up, Bill, before it's too late . . .

'Evidently referring to those,' Willis added, nodding to the newspapers on the desk.

Henshaw nodded and picked them up. Scanning through them he looked chiefly at the dates. When he had examined them — six in all — he frowned, and then went through them again.

'One missing,' he said. 'The issues are consecutive save for one. The issue for December seventh isn't here.'

Willis shrugged. 'Must have got missed somewhere.'

'But why should it? Every other issue is here except that one.' Henshaw put the papers down on the desk again. 'Now why did Barridge put all these papers, and the letters and betting cards in one particular drawer and then lock it? Each item — newspapers, the 'Jenny' letters, the brother's letters, and the betting cards, seems to have some connection with the other. For that reason I think that the missing issue may be important. We have two people in Australia who concern us deeply — James Barridge and Centinel Carr. Both of them are in Melbourne, and these papers are Melbourne weeklies.'

'Significant enough, perhaps,' Willis conceded. 'Funny thing, but I once got the idea that James Barridge and Centinel Carr may be one and the same person. Just a guess. And that Jennifer Carr is working out some complicated scheme of revenge.'

'Anything's possible,' Henshaw said. 'Meantime I've got to have a copy of this December seventh issue of the *Herald* airmailed to me right away. James Barridge said he would be sending them every week, so to find one missing just doesn't make sense. Can't do any harm to find out what was in it, anyway. Send a cable right away to the *Melbourne Herald* and tell them to airmail the December seventh issue.'

Willis nodded and turned to the telephone, began dictating the cable. When he had finished, Henshaw gave a nod.

'Good! Whether there is anything important in these other issues, I don't know yet, and I haven't the time to look now. I — Come in,' Henshaw called out, and the sergeant-in-charge entered with a report sealed in an envelope.

'From the Crayley forensic department, sir,' he announced, and putting the envelope on the desk he turned and went out.

As he read the report a look of profound interest crossed Henshaw's face. Willis looked over his shoulder and read with him:

Micro-analysis of dirt removed from under fingernails of William Barridge deceased reveals tobacco dust, traces of red phosphorus (presumably from match heads), fine yellow blanket hairs (presumable from bed-clothes), one or two fibres from string and slight shreds of carbolic soap. Otherwise nails are clean, as one would expect in a sedentary worker.

'No reference at all to traces of a blue serge suit or a fur coat,' Willis commented. 'That's a bit of a poser! Unless he was so weak-kneed that he really did die without putting up a fight for it.'

'The man or woman who'll die without putting up a fight for life just isn't born, Willis,' the superintendent answered. 'This, in its way, does a good deal to clear the fogs of suspicion hanging round Minton and Mrs. Carr — and it gives me the dim beginnings of an answer to all this. I'm thinking of those slight shreds of carbolic soap.'

Willis gave a start. 'Why — you mean the soap that vanished? From the washroom at Minton's?'

'I do, yes. Sally Higson wanted it for her stocking and couldn't find it. Of course it's quite possible that Barridge used carbolic soap at home, but for the moment I'm going to consider instead whether he got the shreds of carbolic soap from the *washroom* soap, upon which soap he could have taken a key impression as easily as on wax. The soap vanished last Thursday. Today is Tuesday.'

'And soap still under the nails?' Willis questioned. 'Bit of a long time for it to remain, isn't it?'

'Not for soap. It sticks like glue, and remember it would not look like dirt if Barridge inspected his nails. Dissolved soap becomes white. It's quite possible fine shreds of it could remain there for quite a time. From now on,' Henshaw decided, 'I'm going to work on an entirely new tack.'

From the various papers on the desk he selected the betting cards, put them in his pocket and then got to his feet.

'First move in the 'new tack' is to see this bookie, Bob King,' he announced. 'While I'm gone, get those statements typed out for Mrs. Barridge, Mr. Minton, and Mrs. Carr — or is hers finished?'

'Not quite, sir. Soon fix it up.'

With a new light in his eye, the superintendent left and went outside to his car. Before very long he was entering the small premises of 'Sporting Bob

King', Turf Accountant — a big, brawny individual with a sallow complexion and a suspicious look.

'Good morning,' King greeted shortly. 'Sit down, will you? What have I done now?'

'Your business is no concern of mine, Mr. King,' Henshaw answered him. 'I'm here for an entirely different reason, to enquire about one of your clients. These cards are yours, I think?'

The bookie took them and scowled at them. 'Yes, they're mine all right. I issue them to most of my clients, usually at the beginning of the flat season. But these are for last year.'

'I know. They were in the possession of William Barridge.'

Sporting Bob King gave a start. 'William Barridge! The chap who was murdered?'

'That's right, and I'm anxious to find out how long he was a client of yours.'

'As far as I remember . . . ' Bob King reached out to a worn ledger on a shelf beside him, and turned its leaves slowly, ' . . . he never *was* a client of mine. He never placed any bets with me, superintendent. I never heard of him — before I read about him in the papers, that is.'

'You're perfectly sure?'

'Dead sure. Unless, of course, he placed his bets under some other name. Can't think why he'd need to, though. I'm a fully licensed turf accountant and there's no call for hanky-panky like that as far as I'm concerned . . . unless he wanted to keep things quiet because of somebody else.'

'Thanks very much, Mr. King.' Henshaw took the cards back. 'Nothing more I need to know. Good morning.'

Henshaw drove back to the police station and went into the detective-sergeant's office to find him typing out the statements.

'Nothing turned up here sir,' Willis said. 'How about the bookmaker?'

'No sign of Barridge ever having been a client of his.' As Willis looked puzzled, Henshaw added: 'It's logical. If my new plan of action is on the right lines it's just what I expected. See how it develops. Carry on with those statements. I'm going into my office to try and get a few things into focus.'

He went in and settled at the desk. Thinking hard and referring to the various notes he had made at intervals he began to write his observations in full, a method he invariably adopted when he found his mental mechanism in danger of getting clogged with too many possibilities:

1. William Barridge read the racing page while breakfast was being prepared. According to his wife he only started doing this — as far as she can remember — about a fortnight or three weeks ago. I am inclined to think a fortnight.
2. He had racing cards for last year and yet was not a client of the bookmaker concerned.
3. He had a suicide clause inserted in his insurance two weeks before he died.
4. According to Mrs. Jennifer Carr he first made her acquaintance two weeks before he died.

5. According to Mrs. Barridge her husband made a will but she can find no trace of it.

6. He was aware, through Dr. Blandish, that he had contracted endocarditis, but took no steps to alleviate the trouble. At least not through Dr. Blandish.

7. His wife and he were obviously at loggerheads.

8. In spite of a fight for life, of which there is — or was — every evidence in Minton's office, there is no trace of Barridge having clutched at his attacker — that is, Minton, Mrs. Carr, or maybe Standish. Fingernail analysis suggests that he did not clutch at anybody. The analysis does show traces of carbolic soap, however.

9. Jennifer Carr took love letters to Barridge. The address in them has been cut off, the envelopes (which would have betrayed postmark and date) destroyed, and they were found in Barridge's private drawer instead of in a file in his office.

10. Also in this drawer were copies of the Melbourne Herald. One copy for December 7 is missing. In the normal way it would have reached him about the same time (or perhaps a little before this) as he met Mrs. Carr.

11. Barridge knew for some time in advance that Minton was Intending to go to Liverpool. But nobody else did.

12. In spite of being considered a 'mouse' it looks as though Barridge apparently had another woman in his life (Jennifer Carr).

Make-up of William Barridge: Reticent, quiet, and could not change his nature. Never amounted to anything, but worshipped a brother who has achieved a prominent position in Australia. Never forgot a slight. Did he forget that Jennifer Carr (if she spoke the truth) repulsed him? I doubt it! Did he accept the contempt of others, including his family, with good grace? Again, I doubt it! Did he really love his wife? Yet again — I doubt it! He was, it appears, a man with an unusually keen sense of smell, which if I remember correctly from Smith's 'Psychology of a Criminal' may be important.

He was concerned enough about his health to read up the details in a bulky 'Home Doctor' (so says his wife), yet not concerned enough to have a doctor put him right when he contracted endocarditis. From which I infer that the 'Home Doctor' might have had a much deeper meaning for him.

Up to now I freely admit that I have been in something of a fog, but I am inclined to think that the fog has been produced by my getting off on the wrong foot. Now, with my new approach, based on the fingernail analysis, I shall work in a totally different direction, and I am gratified by the results of my first move, namely, that William Barridge had no dealings with Bob King.

I now need to determine the age of the letters sent to Barridge, or else to

*Centinel Carr, by Jennifer; to dis-
cover the reason for the bent
hair-grip; to find the owner of the
star-brooch; and to make sure why
Henry Minton is so obstinately
determined not to give an alibi. I
remain more convinced than ever
now that it is for a reason totally
apart from the murder of Barridge.*
Cherchez la femme: *If I have to seek
a woman at all and fit her into this
case, I believe I need look no farther
than Jennifer Carr. She is without
doubt the pivot about which the
ingenious scheme revolves.*

★ ★ ★

Henshaw sat back in his chair to read the
notes he had made, deciding how many
of them should be conveyed to the Chief
Constable in the form of a report. Then
he glanced up as the sergeant-in-charge
came in, holding — to Henshaw's
astonishment — the hand of a little girl.

'This little lady wants to see you, sir,'
he explained, grinning.

218

'Why, Lucy Barridge!' Henshaw got up quickly. 'Well, Lucy — come in.'

'Yes, sir,' the child assented timidly, and advanced while she looked up under her eyes. When she reached the desk she put an envelope on it upon which had been scrawled the words *Superintendent Henshaw, Hadlam Police Department*.

'Mummy said I was to give you this,' the child explained. 'And I'm to see if there's an answer.'

'And you brought it instead of one of your brothers, eh?' Henshaw smiled, tearing open the envelope.

'Mummy says I've more sense than they have,' the child answered calmly.

The superintendent sat down at the desk again and read the brief note Emily Barridge had penned to him . . .

Dear Superintendent,
After you had left and I turned out the chest of drawers properly I found the enclosed at the back of the drawer which had been locked. I just don't know what it means, but maybe you will. I thought you ought to have it

right away so I'm sending Lucy with it.
Yours sincerely,
Emily Barridge.

The enclosure comprised a thin sheet of copy paper of the type usually used for taking carbons of letters. Henshaw unfolded it and read it through, disguising the astonishment he felt.

January 27th, 1947.
Dear Mr. Minton,
I do not propose to wait much longer for the money you owe me. £1,000 is a lot of money to a man like me, and I mean to have it. I'll wait until this time next week — no more. If I don't get it by next Monday, February 3rd, I'll expose the whole thing, and you know what will be the outcome of that!
Respectfully,
William Barridge.

'Is there any answer, sir?' the child asked.

'Er — no,' Henshaw replied, smiling again. 'You just thank your mother and

say I'll attend to it. Good-bye, Lucy
— and thanks for coming.'

Henshaw hardly heard her leave as the
sergeant showed her out. It was the
arrival of Willis, at the end of typing the
statements for Minton, Mrs. Carr, and
Emily Barridge, which made him glance
up.

'Those are done now, sir,' the detective-
sergeant reported. 'Are we taking them to
be signed or shall we have the respective
parties come here and do it?'

'Never mind them for the moment,'
Henshaw said. 'Read this. Mrs. Barridge
just sent it over — found it after we'd
gone.'

The detective-sergeant read it through
swiftly. His eyes gleamed.

'Here's our motive, sir! Blackmail!
Barridge knew something about Minton
and was going to expose him yesterday
— February third. Before the exposure
could take place Minton murdered
Barridge.'

'That,' Henshaw admitted, 'is certainly
how it looks. And a few hours ago I might
have believed it myself, but if I do so now

I'm liable to upset my new theory. What I am going to do is see Minton himself. I'll take his statement along with me and get it signed. In fact, you'd better come, too, Willis. Let's be going.'

They reached Minton's office just before lunchtime. Everything was apparently going on normally, the entire staff being present and unusually industrious. It was the office boy who showed the two men into Minton's abode, and he motioned to chair.

'Sit down, gentlemen. I take it you are still hunting me for an alibi?'

'Something has happened, Mr. Minton, which makes it imperative that I question you again, and — if possible — show you how vital it is that you prove your alibi. In the course of my investigation this came to light amongst Barridge's effects at his home.'

Henshaw laid the carbon-copy letter on the desk, retaining a hold of one end of it. The solicitor read it through with growing amazement.

'What the devil does this mean?' he demanded furiously.

'I was hoping, Mr. Minton, that you would be able to explain that yourself.'

'How on earth can I? Dammit, I think the man must have gone insane before he died! From this one would imagine that I have some guilty secret of which he knew — that I was being blackmailed into paying a thousand pounds by yesterday in order to preserve the secret. I never heard of such infernal rubbish!'

'You are sure,' Henshaw asked deliberately, 'that you have not got the original of this copy letter?'

'How could I have when I don't know anything about it?' Minton looked at the carbon-copy letter again and then added: 'This is our carbon-copy paper, by the way, and this machine is the one used by Miss Higson. That slanting 'f' is its trademark.'

Henshaw returned the letter to his wallet. 'Since you are a legal man Mr. Minton, I hardly need to remind you that I must have absolute proof of your statement. Frankly, I believe you — but that is obviously not enough. It now looks as though William Barridge was murdered yesterday morning before he could speak, and naturally there seems to be only one person who had the *desire* to silence him. Yourself. That is how a jury would look at it, anyway. You have only one course, and that is to state truthfully where you were at the time of Barridge's death.'

'I told you, man! I was in Liverpool, on the way to see Anstruther.' And as Henshaw smiled faintly the solicitor snapped, 'Don't you believe me?'

'I believe that you invented that story on the spur of the moment — which is one reason why I have not been at any particular trouble to check the alibi as yet. I did make an effort last night and was told that Gerald Anstruther would be away until teatime today. I got his private address from the directory — a thing that you, too, could easily have done, seeing that he is a close friend of yours.'

Henshaw looked across the desk intently. 'Can't you see, sir, that I'm trying to *help* you?'

Minton played needlessly with a bundle of deeds on the blotter. 'Last night,' he said, with a hard smile, 'I told my wife that you are a smart man — and I'm still sure of it. That Liverpool alibi *was* an excuse. I didn't go to Liverpool. I went to London, on private business. Very private. You understand?'

'To see whom?' Henshaw enquired.

'Well, I saw quite a few people, really . . . ' Minton made an effort as if he were throwing everything overboard. 'There was David Elsworth, the manufacturer, Sidney Grayham, the steel man, Kenneth Wilson, the financier . . . Quite a few of them. We met in a party at the Braydock Hotel. I left here at ten-thirty, taking the London train, and got into London about half-past twelve . . . Since we are in the Midlands in Hadlam here it is about the same distance to London as it is to Liverpool. At one-thirty I was having lunch with these men I've mentioned, at which time, so you said, Barridge was murdered.'

Willis made a note of the names involved — in fact, of all Minton's words — and a grim expression slowly spread over Henshaw's face.

'Why didn't you say so in the first

place?' he demanded. 'Obstructing the police isn't exactly a sensible thing to do!'

'I — I know, but I had a reason.' Minton looked genuinely worried. 'All I ask is that once you've verified from one or other of these men that I lunched with them you will question my business no further.'

'I'm not in a position to make promises of that sort, Mr. Minton. Naturally, though, I am only interested in the case I'm handling . . . You say that Barridge, and nobody else, knew you were going to Liverpool. Did he know you were going to Liverpool — or *London?*'

'I said Liverpool.' Minton stopped, shook his dark head and sighed. 'Just the same I wouldn't be a bit surprised if he knew where I was really going. When a man has been your head clerk for twenty years there isn't much he doesn't know about you. Besides, I sometimes let quite a lot of things slip — usually when I have had more to drink than is good for me. All things considered, I haven't the least doubt but what Barridge knew a good deal about me that he never would have known but for — for my weakness. Devil of it is I can't be sure. I never can remember if I've said anything.'

'Supposing, then, that he had heard something he shouldn't, might it have been worth a thousand pounds to you to keep it quiet?'

Minton recognized the quietly worded question for what it was — a trap, and he did not answer it. With a thoughtful smile Henshaw took out the typed record of Minton's earlier statement.

'Whilst I'm here, sir, you might read through this and then sign it. Just initial the pages as you go along. Any alterations you want made can be fixed, of course. I'll let you have a further statement later of what you have said just now.'

While the solicitor read the statement through, Henshaw looked towards the window, towards the filing cabinets, then at the tall lath in the corner for drawing the curtains — or so Arthur Standish had said. His eyes lingered on it for a moment.

'Yes, that seems to be correct,' Minton said, signing the last sheet and initialling the others. 'What I have said since changes things a little, though.'

Henshaw took up the signed statement and put it away again; then he brought out the star brooch and laid it on the blotter. 'Ever seen this before?'

'No.' Minton examined it. 'But it's very pretty — and expensive, too, I'd say. Whose is it?'

'That's what I'm trying to find out.' Henshaw returned it to his pocket and the solicitor hesitated over a comment. Finally, he made it.

'About this business of Carr v. Carr,' Minton said. 'I've made a point of asking my office staff about it. I just couldn't *believe* that Barridge would take a case on his own shoulders without consulting me; but it seems he must have done. In the caller's book is Mrs. Carr's name — twice. She's been here all right in the last fortnight, and Barridge saw her. No doubt of that. I've looked through his business diary to see if there's any reference to her, but there isn't. It's a most extraordinary state of affairs.'

'Yes, isn't it?' Henshaw gave a grim

smile. 'Well, that's all for now, Mr. Minton. I'll get in touch with you if necessary. Thanks for the information.'

He nodded to the detective-sergeant and they went out into the enquiry office. Taking the star brooch from his pocket Henshaw held it forward in his palm. 'Have any of you ever seen this before?' he asked.

Standish looked up from his desk, stared at the brooch, then shook his head. The office boy contented himself with a loud whistle and made no comment. Sally Higson, however, went into sudden ecstasies.

'Oh, it's *lovely!* Beautiful!' Sally stopped, a surprised look on her chunky face. 'Just a minute, inspector. I seem to remember something about it . . . '

She dived her hand into the drawer of her desk and yanked a handbag into view. After searching through it earnestly she finally brought forth a little memo book.

'Star-shape, made up in rubies and garnets . . . ' She was talking half to herself. 'It must belong to Mrs. Carr. You know, the lady that Mr. Minton's been asking us about. On the second time she came here she asked if she had dropped such a brooch in here as it was the only place where she could think of having lost it. We hadn't seen it so she gave me the description in case it happened to turn up. I wrote the details in my memo book here.'

'I see.' Henshaw studied the brooch in his palm. 'That was very sensible of you, Miss Higson, and the information is useful. I'll see that the rightful owner gets it back.'

He pocketed the brooch and then asked another question. 'Do any of you here know if Mr. Barridge made a will? His own will, I mean. One of you might have witnessed it. You, Mr. Standish, for instance.'

The junior clerk shook his head. 'I can't recall ever having witnessed a will on behalf of Mr. Barridge.'

'Neither can I,' Sally added. 'And certainly Jimmy wouldn't do as a witness because he's a minor.'

'Suppose you had witnessed such a will,' Henshaw asked, 'would you know the contents of it?'

'No,' Standish replied. 'The law demands that we witness the *signature* of the testator. The rest of the will form is folded over so that it can't be read by the witness.'

Henshaw shrugged over something and then turned to the door. 'Much obliged. Good morning.' With Willis he returned to the car.

'I don't quite see the reason for your concern about the will, sir,' Willis remarked as they reached the car.

'It's just to verify my conclusions. Mrs. Barridge is reasonably convinced that her husband *did* make a will. If it cannot be found it is no more than I expect — following out the theory I have in mind, that is. Evidently he had somebody apart from the office witness it.'

'Evidently.' Willis could not quite see where all this was leading, but he asked no further questions.

'Somewhere before,' Henshaw said, frowning, 'I've heard the name of Sidney Grayham, the steel king — and as I remember it was in connection with something pretty unsavoury. When I get back to the office I'll ring up the Criminal Records Office at the Yard and see what they've got. I'll wager there's something criminally significant attaching to that gentleman. Not often my memory lets me down.'

'You mean then that Minton is mixing up with criminals? Doesn't look too good for his alibi.'

'I'm pretty sure that Sidney Grayham's activities are open to question — or were, anyhow. As to the other two men I don't know. I'll check on that alibi to the hilt once I've seen Mrs. Carr. At the moment we had better drop in at the Crescent for lunch, and then carry on to Mrs. Carr's afterwards.'

11

At half-past two Jennifer Carr admitted the two men into her small, pleasant flat in Lexhall Mansions. It was the kind of place Henshaw had privately expected of such an essentially feminine woman.

Jennifer Carr herself, in a cornflower blue frock that showed off her blonde attractiveness to perfection, motioned the two men to easy chairs, then went over to the chesterfield and settled herself gracefully.

'I'm sorry to have to bother you again, Mrs. Carr,' Henshaw apologized. 'In the first place, though, I think you should know that despite an extensive search, in which Mr. Minton has joined, there is no trace anywhere in the files of your divorce action against your husband, and Mr. Minton himself knows nothing of it. It seems Mr. Barridge never mentioned it to him.'

'That I can understand, since Mr.

Barridge told me himself that he alone arranged the preliminary details. But there must be some sign of the case in the files! You've perhaps missed it somehow?'

'On the contrary. You gave Mr. Barridge three early love letters, I understand?'

'Yes . . . ' The woman's clear grey-blue eyes opened wide. 'Good heavens, don't tell me you can't find those, either! I don't like those letters lying about where anybody might find them.'

'From what address were they written?'

'From my old address in Kensington where I was staying when I first met Cent — forty-two Rydale Avenue.'

'And what would the dates be?' Henshaw asked.

'Oh . . . ' she waved a hand vaguely. 'They must have been dated somewhere in November nineteen forty-four, since that is when I first became engaged. I was married three months afterwards.'

'Are you sure that you put the date?' Henshaw enquired, and the woman gave a little start.

'As a matter of fact, I'm not. I'm a bit

silly that way, really. I very often put just the day. I have trouble remembering what date it is.'

'A foolish habit,' Henshaw told her, quiet reproof in his voice. 'Besides, such letters lose their value when the date isn't mentioned. For that reason I cannot see why Mr. Barridge thought they would be of use in a divorce suit. However, maybe he knew what he was doing. Er — you said you took them to him when he first suggested he would like all the evidence he could get concerning your first amorous emotions towards your husband?'

'That's right,' Jennifer Carr assented. 'He didn't ask for letters, only evidence. I took the letters of my own free will, and when he saw them he said they were just what he wanted.'

Henshaw drew them from his uniform jacket pocket and put them on the arm of the chesterfield at the woman's elbow.

'These they, Mrs. Carr?'

'Why, yes, these are they — !' Then she paused with a little murmur of dismay as she examined them. Her azurine eyes looked suddenly into the superintendent's.

'Who cut off the tops?' she demanded in astonishment. 'There should be my embossed Rydale Avenue address on these! What good are they when they're mutilated like this?'

'They weren't found in a file in Mr. Minton's office, but in a private drawer in Barridge's home. And they were in exactly the condition you see them in now.'

The woman simply stared, uncomprehending.

'Which,' Henshaw went on, 'makes it possible to deduce certain facts — namely, that those letters were sent to Mr. *Barridge*, exclusively from you, and he kept them.'

Jennifer Carr jumped to her feet indignantly, flung the letters down fiercely on the chesterfield. 'I resent that!' she snapped, anger colouring her cheeks. 'They were written to my husband, a little over two years ago. Think what you like, but that's the absolute truth!'

'You did remark, Mrs. Carr, that Mr. Barridge made advances to you,' Henshaw commented, unmoved.

The woman swung on him angrily. 'He *did!* And I told him what I thought about him, too. I've told you already how I rejected his advances.'

'I know, but of course I have only your word for it that the matter ended there.' Then as Henshaw saw another torrent of words forming he raised a hand. 'You see,' Henshaw explained, hunching forward in his chair, 'it doesn't matter in the least to me, *personally*, whether you and Mr. Barridge had an affectionate regard for each other or not. My sole concern is to find a murderer and protect the innocent. From the viewpoint of the law, letters signed by you and discovered in Barridge's private drawer have been found. The 'Dear Snookums . . . ' could be — in fact would be — interpreted as meaning him. You have also said you were 'out with him in public on two occasions'; a jury would weigh that fact up from every aspect. Summing it up, it would look from the angle of circumstantial evidence as though the divorce proceedings were merely a blind and that you really had some kind of amorous entanglement with Barridge.'

'Well, I didn't!' Jennifer Carr retorted stubbornly. 'You've seen Barridge: you see me. Do you think such a thing could even be possible?'

Henshaw took the three letters back and pocketed them. 'Tell me something.' The superintendent evaded the question. 'For what reason did your husband leave you?'

'We . . . quarreled. It was a furious, bitter quarrel while it lasted and there just didn't seem to be any way in which we could patch it up afterwards. My husband simply left me, high and dry, and I couldn't find out where he had gone. Nor did I, until he wrote me from Australia, even though I asked the police for help. That was when I decided to sue for a divorce.'

'And you said he wrote you from Melbourne. Have you his letter? I'd rather like to see it. I shan't use it in the case unless it has a direct bearing upon it. You can be assured of that.'

'You can see it with pleasure,' Jennifer

Carr assented, and getting to her feet she went to the bureau by the window. 'I showed it to Mr. Barridge, of course, so that he could see everything was above board.'

'Oh, you did?' Henshaw reflected over the fact for a moment but passed no comment.

For a while the woman searched the bureau and then brought the letter to view and handed it across. The envelope was stamped 'Melbourne, Australia' and postmarked December 2, 1946. Henshaw took out the letter and read it carefully:

236 N. Elizabeth Street,
Melbourne, Australia.
December 2nd, 1946.
Dear Jenny,
This will no doubt surprise you. I have been here quite a few months now. After I left you I spent quite twelve months getting my passport fixed and arranging for a boat on which to travel. I think it much better that we stay apart than go through life forever warring with each other. You have plenty of

*money and a spirit too independent for
my liking. That initial blow-up we had
showed me just which way the wind
was going. We're just temperamentally
unsuited to each other, though we
neither of us knew it, apparently, when
we married.*

*You will not hear from me ever again,
but I thought it only fair to let you
know where you stand. If you want to
take action for divorce, do so. I shan't
contest it.*

In remembrance,
Cen.

'So your money and independent spirit
was the main cause of the trouble?'
Henshaw murmured, and Jennifer Carr
nodded soberly.

'I'm afraid so.'

'This is an unusual sort of letter.'
Henshaw looked through it again. 'In
fact, it sounds as if conscience was the
main thing which prompted your husband to write it.'

'I rather got that impression, too,'
Jennifer Carr admitted. 'In fact it sounds

almost like a last will and testament. Those phrases: 'you will never hear from me again,' and 'In remembrance' make it sound just like that. But probably I'm guessing at things! Anyway, he has at least had the decency to let me know where I stand.'

'Yes, indeed.' Henshaw returned the letter to her, his face thoughtful. For the moment his mind had strayed to the missing December 7th issue of the *Melbourne Herald*. 'A little while ago, Mrs. Carr, you lost a star-shaped brooch, I believe, and mentioned the fact to Miss Higson in Minton's' office?'

'Yes, that's right.'

Henshaw took it from his pocket and laid it in the woman's palm. 'There it is — I think?'

She nodded slowly, gazing at it. 'This is it, all right. The clasp is loose, which is why I must have lost it. I really must get it seen to. It's both valuable and sentimental; it belonged to my mother.'

Jennifer Carr's eyes raised to Henshaw's. 'Where did you find it?'

'In a pocket of Mr. Barridge's jacket

— the one he was wearing when he met his death.'

'But — but I told him on my last visit there — about a week ago — that I'd lost my brooch on my previous visit and I asked him if he'd seen it. He denied all knowledge of it. Then I asked the staff. They hadn't seen it, either, but Miss Higson took down the particulars and promised to keep her eyes open. This means Mr. Barridge must have lied to me.'

'Either that or else he had only just found it and put it in his pocket, where we found it as he lay dead.'

'I could have lost it anywhere, I suppose,' she said, 'but I *do* know I had it on before I went into Barridge's office because my scarf caught on the edge of it and I pulled it free. I'm inclined to think that is when it must have come undone and dropped. And that was in Mr. Barridge's office.'

'In any case I'm glad to have discovered its rightful owner,' Henshaw answered, taking it back from her. 'For the time being I'll retain it, if you don't mind.' He returned the brooch to his pocket and then started off on a different topic.

'What kind of health had your husband, Mrs. Carr? Was he a strong, virile type of man when you knew him two years ago?'

'In every sense of the word.'

'What was his occupation?'

'Engineer. Not particularly high up the ladder, but with very good prospects. On his own account. I expect he has taken up the same profession in Australia.'

'Quite possibly,' Henshaw agreed, reflecting. 'Naturally, he must have been in reasonably good health to have secured permission to emigrate. The authorities are strict on that kind of thing these days. I just wondered in view of his peculiar letter to you — with its definitely 'last gesture' aspect — if he knew he might die and meant to make a clean breast of everything before he did so.'

The superintendent scowled meditatively at the carpet, then he slowly shook his head. 'Barridge conducted your divorce case in the weirdest way, Mrs. Carr,' he said at length. 'By rights he should immediately have made contact with your husband in Australia in order to substantiate the facts, and yet there is not the least sign of him having done so. Any letters he might have sent should surely have been typed by Miss Higson — and even if, failing that, Barridge typed them himself he would have been bound to retain a copy.'

'It looks,' the woman said impatiently, 'that he didn't do a thing about it. Incidentally, what am I supposed to do now about my divorce? Do I hand it over to Mr. Minton, or — what?'

'There is just a chance that by waiting for a while — as, indeed, you will have to do until the Barridge case is over — you might be able to save yourself a good deal of expense concerning this divorce case. In fact, you may not even have to institute it. I have the impression, Mrs. Carr, that — though you don't know it definitely at the moment — you are a widow!'

12

Upon returning to headquarters Henshaw learned that the inquest on Barridge would be held the following morning in Crayley.

'And we'll ask for an adjournment until our enquiry's over,' he said briefly to Willis. 'Now . . . ' He settled at the desk. 'I've a cable to send to Australia, Willis. Grab your notebook.'

The detective-sergeant obeyed, wishing he could see a little more clearly from what angle his superior was working.

'*The Chief of Police, Melbourne,*' Henshaw said, pondering the letters and notes he had taken from his pocket. 'Er . . . *Contact Centinel Carr of two thirty-six Elizabeth Street, Melbourne. Ask him if he wrote letter to his wife Jennifer, dated December second last year. Also ask him if his wife wrote three love letters to him in November, nineteen forty-four, before they were married, one* of them as follows and addressed from forty-two Rydale Avenue, Kensington — Quote, Dear Snookums, such love as ours is something I never thought could exist. If our married life is destined to be as perfect as the bliss we know now we shall be fortunate indeed. I shall count the hours until we next meet. Your loving Jenny. Unquote. Cable answer at earliest. Henshaw, Superintendent, Hadlam Police, Hadlam, England ... And get that off right away.'

Willis nodded and turned to the telephone. Whilst he was busy dictating it, Henshaw pressed the button for the sergeant-in-charge and handed him the love letters in a sealed envelope.

'Have these sent over to the forensic department in Crayley,' he said, 'and have them find out how old the ink is. Ask them to hurry it up.'

'Yes, sir.' The sergeant departed.

'Now — Sidney Grayham,' Henshaw muttered. 'Let's see what we can find out about him.'

He yanked the telephone to him and had the operator put him on to the

Criminal Records Department of Scotland Yard.

'Henshaw here — Hadlam police,' he said, as the superintendent of the department answered. 'Would you mind looking through your files and telling me if you have anything on a man named Sidney Grayham? He's in steel, or he is at the moment, anyway . . . Yes, I'll wait.'

The answer came over the line. 'The only thing we have against Sidney Grayham is that he was arrested three years ago on a charge of running contraband — defeating the Customs. There wasn't enough evidence, though, and the case broke down.'

'What is his description?' Henshaw asked.

'Just a moment . . . Five feet seven, stout build, round faced, blue eyed, clean shaven. Hair black, graying at the temples. Do you want a print of his face?'

'No, thanks, that won't be necessary. You've told me all I need to know.'

Henshaw rang off and glanced at the clock, made up his mind about something. 'Take down these particulars;

Willis,' he instructed, and gave Grayham's description as it had been given to him. Then he added: 'I haven't the least doubt but what it is the same Sidney Grayham. Our friend Minton is mixed up in something mighty shady, otherwise he wouldn't be so cagey about giving an alibi. Now he knows he may get the even more serious charge of murder wrapped round his neck if he doesn't speak, I think he has decided to risk everything.'

'I suppose then, that we should go to London and interview Grayham?'

'Yes — and the other two men as well. If it were only a matter of establishing Minton's alibi I could do it over the 'phone, but I'd rather like to know what he's up to. His anxiety to keep me from enquiring into his business definitely intrigues me. There's even just a chance we may clean up two birds with one stone — prove an alibi and discover what Minton's game is at the same time. Hand me that directory of business firms, will you?'

Willis hauled it from the shelf behind him, and within a few minutes Henshaw had got the business addresses of all three men concerned, together with the telephone numbers, then he pondered and frowned.

'Hmmm — blast!' he muttered finally. 'The inquest! I'd forgotten that. We couldn't reach London before late evening at the earliest and that would be far too late to start enquiring. That would mean tomorrow morning, and we've just got to be at Crayley.' He sighed. 'Looks as if I'll have to use the 'phone after all and make a personal trip after the inquest tomorrow if I need.'

He glanced at the clock again. 'I'll give Minton a bit more time yet to get back from lunch, then I'll ask him for Grayham's description and see if it tallies with the one in the Criminal Records.'

He got to his feet and walked about the office thoughtfully. 'That confounded hairgrip!' he muttered. 'I just can't see where it fits.'

'Incidentally, sir,' Willis remarked, 'you didn't ask Mrs. Carr if she could tell us anything about it.'

'A hairgrip like that isn't exclusive.

Millions of women in all walks of life use them. If it didn't belong to Mrs. Carr I didn't want her to think some other woman was also involved. Doesn't do to show your hand too much . . . Why was that hairgrip *bent*, Willis? That's the snag!'

Going over to the locker, Henshaw brought the hairgrip from the envelope, and stared at it intently. 'It has been bent on purpose. Not accidentally trodden on, or anything. I'll take it over to the micro-analysts and see if there is anything interesting in it that the naked eye can't detect. Since it won't speak for itself, maybe it can be made to.'

'Good idea, sir. By the way, why did you suggest to Mrs. Carr that she might be a widow?'

'Oh, that!' Henshaw smiled faintly. 'It was pure assumption, really — but, as far as it goes, logical enough. That letter which Carr wrote to Jennifer had a definitely 'last gasp' flavor about it, hadn't it?'

'Well — er — ' Willis hesitated. 'By no means conclusive, sir. Besides, Mrs. Carr said he was a virile, healthy man. Why should he die?'

'Looking at the thing psychologically,' Henshaw went on, meditating, 'it suggests — as I said at the time — that conscience suddenly stabbed him. Conscience doesn't stab people unless they are ill, on hard times, or about to kick this mortal coil. Then, in an effort to atone for past misdeeds, they sometimes do the most extraordinary things. If, indeed, Centinel Carr *did* die, and William Barridge knew about it in advance, it would account for Barridge making no effort to put the divorce suit through or communicate with Carr.'

'But how could he know that?' Willis demanded.

'From one very reliable source — the obituary column, or some such announcement, in the *Mclbourne Herald*.'

'Why — of course!' Willis exclaimed, starting.

'That William Barridge was playing some sort of game of his own seems reasonably certain by now,' Henshaw continued, 'and it is possible that he knew of Centinel Carr's death before Mrs. Carr herself. The paper containing the information could have been the missing one for December seventh, five days after Carr sent off his letter. Sheer chance, I suppose, and nothing else, led Mrs. Carr to Minton's office — maybe because he is reputed to be the best solicitor in town, and she is obviously not without money to pay for the best advice — and Barridge happened to know in advance something which she, apparently, did *not* know. And she still doesn't.

'And if my theory is right it is one of the most vicious and ingenious schemes I've yet come across. We've got to watch every step we make, Willis, and only come to a conclusion very slowly, otherwise we might find ourselves involved in a monstrous miscarriage of justice. Anyhow, let's see what the micro-analysts can find out about the hairgrip.'

They went out to the car and Willis drove them swiftly down the broad highway that connected Hadlam with its much bigger neighbor of Crayley, where the police department maintained a complete forensic laboratory for the county area.

After greeting with the inspector-in-charge, Henshaw and Willis went on their way to the long, glass-roofed room where most of the police work was undertaken. Only two experts were staff workers: what others were needed were called in from their normal occupations as occasion demanded. At the moment the two experts were busy on a routine task, and Superintendent Robert Baines was writing at his desk.

'Hello there, Henshaw!' he greeted, getting up and shaking hands. 'And Willis . . . Come over for a report on those letters? We're on with them now.'

'That wasn't exactly the reason,' Henshaw answered, 'but I'll take a look just the same.'

Baines nodded to the two men working in a corner and they glanced up as Henshaw and Willis looked over their shoulders, where Jennifer Carr's love letters were spread out under the magnifying and other instruments.

'Afraid you'll have to wait a day or two for a report on these, Henshaw,' one of the analysts said, glancing up. 'The answer will be dead right, though; you'll have that satisfaction. Fortunately these letters are written in blue-black ink — nutgall iron tannin compound. Mixed with green vitriol, it's a colourless fluid that darkens by oxidization when exposed to the air. It unites chemically with the paper to form a black iron compound.

'We've just made the first optical test,' the analyst went on. 'Nutgall ink darkens perpetually to a final maximum. The tintometer will show us in a day or two if the ink has changed color and gone darker. If it has, then it is comparatively new. If it hasn't, then it is at least two years old. Two years is about the maximum time taken for nutgall ink to dry to its deepest and final change of color.'

'Who'd be a crook?' Henshaw murmured, grinning. 'Thanks, boys. Let me know what happens the moment you're ready — hopefully before the Chief Constable gets restive. In the meantime can anybody give this the once-over and tell me if there's anything interesting in it?'

He brought the bent hairgrip to view and held it up.

'I'll do that for you myself,' Baines said, taking it and walking across to the nearest binocular-microscope. 'Save taking the boys off their job.'

Henshaw and Willis stood watching interestedly as he adjusted the eyepieces and examined the bent hairgrip in the radiance of a powerful spotlight, which exactly illumined the area beneath the microscope. After a minute examination he straightened up and handed the hairgrip back.

'Part of its surface is badly abraded,' he said. 'Right up to the elbow bend where it turns into the shape of an L. It looks to me as though it has been pushed into something made of wood for halfway up its length, and then bent sharply. There are one or two small slivers of wood, invisible to the naked eye, lodging in the spring section at the end of the grip.'

'Wood, eh?' Henshaw mused over it.

'Any idea what kind of wood?'

'Hard to tell when there's so little of it, but it's rough, unpainted wood of some kind. Afraid that is as far as I can get.'

'Any signs of hairs in the grip?'

'None. In fact I'd say the thing's more or less brand new.'

'Well, thanks anyway,' Henshaw said, 'even if I don't quite get the angle. And do your best to hurry up that tintometer report for me.'

Henshaw and Willis took their leave and returned to the car outside.

'Rough, unpainted wood,' Henshaw repeated, frowning. 'That is a bit of a steep one. Where have we seen anything like that in this business so far? Maybe we'll recall later. Let's get back to headquarters.'

Then, arriving at headquarters, he let the problem sink into his subconscious for the time being, and instead he put a call through to Henry Minton's office.

'Hello, Henshaw,' he said curtly, as he was connected. 'What's wrong now?'

'Nothing much, Mr. Minton. I want a description of Sidney Grayham, that's all.'

'*Description* of him? What on earth for?'

'To help you, as a matter of fact. I want to be sure that I'm getting the right Sidney Grayham. It's not an uncommon name by any means.'

'Oh . . . I see. Well, he's shortish and heavily built, blue eyes, dark hair going grey, and clean shaven.'

'Thanks — I think that will do fine for what I need. Much obliged. Goodbye.' He rang off.

'It's *the* Sidney Grayham, all right, Willis.'

'And by this time,' the detective-sergeant complained, 'Minton has had plenty of opportunity to ask those three men to fix an alibi for him.'

'He's had the time, yes; but I don't think he'll have done that. I think he *was* with them, so why should he *ask* them to say so? We can soon find out.'

The superintendent raised the receiver again and gave the number of Sidney Grayham's steel concern headquarters in London. There was a good deal of hedging on the part of a switchboard girl until she realized that it was the police on the line, then without hesitation she switched through to the industrialist himself. His deep, heavy voice came over the wire.

'Hello? Yes? Grayham speaking. What's this about the police?'

'Superintendent Henshaw speaking, sir, Hadlam police. I have an important enquiry to make of you. It concerns Mr. Henry Minton ... Yes, Minton. He's informed me that he lunched with you and two other gentlemen at the Braydock Hotel yesterday. Can you tell me if that is correct?'

There was a long pause, then: 'I don't know where that notion came from, superintendent, but it's entirely wrong.'

'Wrong?' Henshaw straightened in his chair and a troubled look crossed his face. 'But he is surely correct in saying that you are a business acquaintance of his?'

'Well, in a remote kind of way, yes. I haven't seen him, though, for at least six or seven months.'

'I ... see.' Henshaw spoke the words slowly. 'Well, thank you, Mr. Grayham.

I'm sorry I troubled you.'

'Quite all right. I'm sorry, too, that you seem to have been misinformed.'

The superintendent put the receiver down. He rubbed his chin and then met Willis's glance. He had heard the details through the receiver.

'What do you make of it, sir?' he asked, puzzled.

Henshaw did not attempt an answer to the problem there and then. Picking up the receiver once more, he got through to David Elsworth — after some delay through the line being engaged — and then to Kenneth Wilson. In each case he was fortunate enough to catch both men in their offices. And in each instance their answers were the same: Minton had not lunched with them, though they did not state a time when they had last seen the solicitor.

'Something damned queer here,' Henshaw declared at last, slapping the desk with the flat of his hand. 'Either they really didn't see Minton or else they don't intend to admit the fact.'

'Come to think of it, sir, there was time

before you managed to get Elsworth for Grayham to have telephoned him to keep quiet,' Willis pointed out. 'The line was engaged. Remember? And while you were talking to Elsworth what was there to prevent Grayham telling Wilson to also deny all knowledge of having met Minton?'

'Yes, it's possible,' Henshaw said, taking a deep breath. 'And if it comes to that the reason isn't far to seek. The murder of Barridge has come to the notice of the public through the newspapers. There are few men, especially in a big position, who will lend themselves to any part of a murder business, even if it's only for the purpose of proving an alibi. That, I believe, is the answer.'

'Which makes it that Minton's alibi can't be proved, and also makes it that we've no real idea what he's up to.'

'As to that . . . ' Henshaw considered deeply for several moments. 'I'm going to force his hand,' he said curtly. 'Come with me. I'll probably need a witness.'

When they arrived at the solicitor's place of business he was plainly surprised

— and annoyed — to find them again on his premises.

'I'm getting a bit tired of this sort of thing, superintendent,' he said impatiently. 'First you call, then you telephone, then you call again. How do you suppose I'm ever going to get any work done?'

'I should imagine that you are more concerned with preserving your innocence concerning Barridge than in getting your work done, Mr. Minton,' Henshaw answered curtly. 'I've telephoned the three men you mentioned — Grayham, Wilson, and Elsworth.'

'Good!' Minton sat back in his chair and gave a cynical smile. 'Now you know!'

'That's just it — I don't. Each of them has denied that you lunched with them. Elsworth and Wilson seemed to regard you as something of a stranger, and Grayham said it is six or seven months since he saw you.'

Minton's beefy face went a much deeper tint; then suddenly he slammed his fist down on the desk.

'The damned dirty liars!' he exploded.

'What in hell sort of a game are they trying to pull? Excuse me!' he snapped, and whipped up the telephone receiver. To Sally Higson he rapped out: 'Get me Sidney Grayham of the Grayham Steel Corporation right away. City, six nine o four. Hurry it up, girl!'

Minton sat and glowered, breathing hard. 'Maybe they don't realize how serious this business is.'

'Maybe they do,' Henshaw murmured. 'They know you are mixed up in murder and don't want to alibi for you for fear of getting mixed up in it themselves. Murder is a nasty business whichever way you look at it — and the court proceedings alone are damaging to one's prestige if one happens to be high up in the business world.'

The telephone bell jangled. Minton snatched the instrument up. 'Sidney?' he demanded, and at a squawking response he went on: 'What the blazes do you mean by telling Superintendent Henshaw that I didn't lunch with you yesterday? Eh? Yes, of course he's here. He's just been telling me.'

Henshaw strained forward intently but he could not catch the words in the receiver. Minton listened, fury darkening his face, then he broke in:

'Look here, this situation is desperate! I've got to have that alibi! If I don't, I'm liable to get mixed up with a murder charge. You know by now as well as I do — and the rest of the great British public — that my head clerk was murdered yesterday about the time I was lunching with you . . . You what? Why, you infernal liar, I — '

Minton broke off at a sharp crack in the receiver. Very slowly he put the instrument down and breathed hard.

'What's the matter?' the superintendent asked dryly. 'Won't Mr. Grayham play ball?'

'No . . . No, he won't. But it's lies, I tell you! All lies! I *was* there!'

'Without those three men to prove it, Mr. Minton, your alibi falls to pieces, and I am entitled to place whatever construction I wish on your actions. The blackmail note carbon in Barridge's possession, your lack of an alibi, the fact that you had the chance to return here and do the deed, that you would know when the janitor and staff were absent, your fingerprints on the knife . . . I may have to charge you.'

Minton breathed hard and did not say anything.

'Unless,' Henshaw finished, in a quieter voice, 'you are prepared to tell me the nature of the business you discussed with those three men.'

'I can't. It was strictly private.'

'Or illegal?'

'What?' Minton's sudden wrath was somehow unconvincing.

'Sidney Grayham is not what one would call an upright member of society,' Henshaw said. 'In fact, according to the Criminal Records Office at Scotland Yard he was arrested three years ago on a charge of contraband. The case wasn't proved, but for him to be brought that far the Yard must have been pretty sure. I don't doubt that they slipped up on a legal technicality somewhere . . .

'With Sidney Grayham mixed up in 'private' business I am prepared to gamble that it runs foul of the law. If it is — no matter how bad — it can't be worse than murder. It's up to you, Mr. Minton. Tell me the nature of your business and I'll have the right people enquire into it, and they will take care of it that those other three men are *made* to speak and say if you were with them. Otherwise you may find yourself charged with murder! And once that happens you may not find it so easy to extricate yourself.'

Minton gave a slow, half-crooked smile. 'When I said you were smart, superintendent, I was right,' he sighed. 'You've wangled me into the tightest corner I've ever been in — either divulge my activities or arrest me for murder, with very sound circumstantial evidence to back you up. All right, I'll take a chance — and after the way those three have denied my very existence I'm almost glad to think they'll get it where it hurts most. The answer to my activities can be covered in two words: 'Black Market'.'

'In what form exactly?' Henshaw asked.

'All manner of things — textiles, cigarettes, a great many of the things which are in short supply. Sidney Grayham is the head of the ring, and Wilson and Elsworth are lesser lights. I do the legal side to keep things as much out of trouble as I can. With the evidence I have I could put all three of those men in jail for twenty years, and I'll be damned if I won't after the way they've treated me! I've made a pile of money out of it, even though I did guess it might end disastrously one day. However, I was willing to take that chance.'

'I suspected some form of outside income when I saw your home,' Henshaw commented.

'And when I first saw you nosing about my office I had the fright of my life,' Minton said, with still the same hard smile. 'Not knowing anything about Barridge's murder I was sure that the police had somehow got wind of my activities. That was why I was so upset. I just didn't know *what* to think at first.'

'Tell me something,' Henshaw said, taking little notice of the solicitor's remarks. 'You said the other day that at times you may have given secrets away.

Could Barridge have known of your Black Market activities?'

'He might have done. I've no idea — but he certainly did not blackmail me, in spite of what that carbon-copy letter had to say.'

Henshaw got to his feet. 'I'll send the facts on the Black Market side of things to the Yard and let them deal with it. They will prove your alibi to the hilt, and once they have done that you cease to be of interest to me. A last word of advice,' Henshaw added, as he reached the door. 'Don't try and run away. That would make your alibi all the more difficult. Come on, Willis; we have all we require here.'

★　★　★

Henshaw found the Chief Constable awaiting him when they arrived back in his office.

'Well, Henshaw, any nearer?' he enquired.

'I think so, sir. I'm as good as satisfied that Mr. Minton, suspect number one, did *not* murder Barridge . . . ' For the

Colonel's benefit Henshaw outlined the events concerning Minton up to date. 'So it seems to me,' he continued, 'that no man would willingly admit his connection with a Black Market ring unless he was absolutely certain of saving his neck from a murder charge by so doing. For that reason in particular I am convinced that Minton did not murder Barridge.'

'Yes, sounds reasonable,' the Chief Constable agreed. 'Have you advised the Yard about Minton?'

'No, but I'll do so this very moment if you'll excuse me.'

Henshaw turned to the telephone and after the usual preliminaries was connected with Chief Inspector Slade, a remarkably taciturn but brilliant individual of the C.I.D. with whom he had often discussed a problem. With his usual silence the Chief Inspector listened to the details.

'All right, Henshaw,' he said finally. 'You leave this to me. And those other two you mention — Elsworth and Wilson — are not such innocents abroad as you seem to think. We've had our eye on them for some time in regard to currency regulations etcetera. This may be our chance to land something since you've nailed a member of the organization who is willing to speak. I'll let you know how I get on — either personally or over the 'phone.'

'Thanks,' Henshaw responded. 'Goodbye.' He put the telephone back on its cradle and turned his attention to the Chief Constable once more.

'If you accept the view that Minton is not responsible,' the Colonel said slowly, 'you leave a lot of loose ends lying about, don't you? How about the blackmail carbon-copy letter? How about only Minton's prints being on the knife? If the murderer was *not* Minton how did the murderer — or murderess — manage to keep his or her prints from the hilt and leave Minton's *on*? Certainly gloves couldn't have been used because they would have smudged. And wiping would either wipe all of them away, or none. How do you explain it?'

'I think I may be able to later on, after another examination of the knife by the micro-analysts. For the moment I'd rather leave the matter in abeyance. As for the carbon-copy letter: there are two possible answers. Either Barridge sent it and Minton denies the fact completely — since it doesn't matter much now Barridge is dead; or else Barridge wrote it but never sent the original, retaining only the carbon.'

'But what on earth for?' the Colonel demanded. 'That just doesn't make sense.'

'It might, sir — to a man of Barridge's temperament. It falls into the same group as those people of backward nature who write the most laudable accounts of themselves and then revel in the reflected glory. Since they are *not* important, and can never hope to be, they make themselves so in their imagination. Any psychologist could explain it.'

'That's a bit too high flown for me,' the Chief Constable decided, shrugging. 'I want facts. What's more, I've got to have them, and an arrest — both to satisfy the public and the higher-ups. If you feel that you can't handle this thing then for

Heaven's sake say so and let Scotland Yard take it over.'

'I can handle it, sir,' Henshaw answered confidently. 'I know I'm on the right track, but as far as I can see at present it may take quite a few weeks to sort it all out. If I make any precipitate arrest I may also commit a frightful blunder. I want to be absolutely sure first.'

'Well . . . all right.' Colonel Wilton sighed. 'You're much more closely in touch with this business than I am. Leaving Minton out of it, what comes next? Mrs. Carr?'

'Again, I don't think she did it. I am, of course, aware that the position of the wound in Barridge's back makes it feasible that she could have done it — and the bent hairgrip also points inevitably to a woman. But I can't imagine a woman of Jennifer Carr's type — refined, essentially feminine, doing such a thing.'

'Nobody is a born killer,' the Chief Constable commented. 'The urge comes suddenly, through vast stress of emotion, as a rule. You know that.'

'Yes, sir, I know it; but I'm also a great believer in studying the psychological make-up of a person. Even had I found Jennifer Carr with the knife in her hand I still would not consider her the murderess . . . Looking at the more practical side, there is no trace of her prints on the knife, and, indeed, I haven't even made an effort to get a sample of her prints so convinced am I of her innocence. For another thing I don't think that the motive would be strong enough — the advances of Barridge which she promptly repulsed.'

'With Minton and Mrs. Carr out of the running who else is there? Either some member of the office staff or maybe the janitor, or else an unknown quantity.'

'I think we can leave both Sally Higson and the office boy out of it,' Henshaw answered. 'Standish has had me wondering once or twice, but in his case I'm stumped for a motive, unless one existed between him and Barridge which hasn't been revealed. And Barridge can't reveal it now, and Standish won't.'

'These issues apart,' the Colonel said,

'how did Barridge get into Minton's room when only Minton had the key? I know that you have said Barridge could have taken an impression of the key, probably on a piece of carbolic soap from the washroom, but in that case what became of the key? Shouldn't the key have been among his effects? If he didn't know he was going to be murdered — and presumably he didn't — he wouldn't be at any particular pains to rid himself of the duplicate key. So where has it gone?'

'Certainly it wasn't among his effects,' Henshaw muttered. 'Nor was it in his own office or the general office — '

He stopped, struck by a sudden thought. Seemingly suddenly unaware of either the Chief Constable or Willis he pulled his notes from his pocket and searched through them, then from his desk drawer he took the photograph of the office in which Barridge had been found.

'I believe I've got something, sir!' he exclaimed. 'As I told you, I had this bent hairgrip under the microscope and found that it has traces of wood slivers in it — rough, unpainted wood. Into the wood the hairgrip was jammed up to the L-bend. In the office — here's the photograph — there is one thing which fits the rough wood description — the long lath with which Minton draws the curtains over the window.'

Willis gave a start. 'That would fit it exactly! But just what are you getting at, sir?'

'Just this: If the bent grip were jammed in the end of the lath it would resemble a hook, wouldn't it? Very well, suppose the duplicate Yale key were hanged on that hook, by the hole in the key-top, and the lath was then lowered out of Minton's office window? The key could be jolted off so as to fall into the drain in the centre of the yard below, and that is one hiding-place where nobody would ever think of looking for it.'

'But why?' Wilton furrowed his brow. 'Why on earth didn't the murderer simply take it away and save all that trouble?'

'Because it's open to doubt if the murderer *had* the duplicate. That's the whole point. Barridge had the duplicate key and to absolutely rid himself of it it's possible he used the method I have described. The end of the lath would easily reach the drain from the first-floor window. By that expedient he could avoid the risk of just tossing the key out of the window and trusting to luck it would go down the drain. He hung it right over the drain and then jerked the key into it. The hook, or rather the hair-grip, also came off and fell in the yard, though whether that was accidental or deliberate I just don't know at this stage.'

'Couldn't Barridge have gone down into the yard and done the thing properly? Why all the hocus-pocus?'

'Because I believe he didn't want to be seen leaving the office, as he certainly would have been, by the janitor. Nor would it have been any use him jumping into the yard because he could not have got back, except by entering the front of the building. The yard is not overlooked, so nobody would have seen him at work with the lath. There is the possibility that the hairgrip was put there deliberately, after it had served its original purpose, in order to turn guilt in the direction of a woman — namely, Mrs. Carr.'

'You mean, then, that Barridge deliberately let himself into Minton's office, disposed of the duplicate key in the way you've outlined, and then . . . What? Who killed him? His next caller was presumably Mrs. Carr. You suggest that he put that hairgrip in the yard to make guilt attach to her?'

'Possibly so. He had had the opportunity to notice what kind of hairgrip she uses — and they are identical to the one we found. Only the one *we* found has never been used in the hair. It's brand new. Barridge could easily have bought a few of the grips from a woman's hairdresser's. In fact, since the L-grip is a new one I think that is just what he did do.'

'But why?' the Colonel insisted. 'If he did all that he must have known that he was going to *be* murdered!'

'I believe he did know, and made things look as though either Minton or Mrs. Carr had done it. We've found evidence enough to point to either of them, and — with all due modesty — maybe a less careful investigator would have arrested one or other of them by now on the facts. That is why I say I must watch every step I make before I arrive at a definite conclusion.'

'But why was the evidence slanted towards Mrs. Carr? What had Barridge against her?'

'She had repulsed him, sir,' Henshaw replied quietly. 'A case of 'a man scorned' instead of a woman. I have been assured from various sources that, quiet though he was, Barridge was the kind of man who never forgot a slight, and think that that rejection wounded his vanity enormously. As far as I have progressed up to now, I think the villain we are seeking is not so much the murderer of William Barridge as William Barridge himself. There's still a long way to go but I'll gamble it will turn out to be a unique situation when all the facts are clear.'

With a grave smile Henshaw got to his feet. 'I fancy,' he added, 'that Mr. Minton is going to have several kinds of a fit when we turn up at his office yet again. But I've got to see that lath and clear out the drain in the yard. We may find the key. If we do then that point is proven and we're that much farther along the road.'

The Chief Constable rose also. 'Good enough — and let me know how you get on. Do I take it that you are, in a sense, building up a picture of William Barridge by which you hope to arrive at the right answer?'

'That's it, sir,' Henshaw assented. 'I've already had many illuminating sidelights on his nature. When I have all of them I'll see what sort of a composite they produce.'

The Chief Constable strolled with the two men to the door. 'You've got me thinking of suicide again as the answer,' he said, reflecting. 'Even so, I can't see how. As you yourself remarked, for a man to stab himself in the back and keep the blade level he would have to have the body of a contortionist!'

'Or the mind of one,' Henshaw responded.

13

The reappearance of Henshaw and Willis in his office towards the close of the afternoon was accepted by Minton with a resigned calm.

'What about those men who are to prove my alibi?' Minton asked. 'Have you done anything more about it?'

'I've informed Chief Inspector Slade of Scotland Yard. I don't doubt you'll be hearing from him: in fact you'll probably be receiving a visit.'

'The sooner I'm cleared of this business concerning Barridge the better I'll like it — even if it does mean trouble from another direction. Anyway, what do you want with mc this time?'

'With you personally, nothing,' the superintendent told him. 'I just want to have a good look at that lath with which you draw the curtains.'

The solicitor sat watching as Henshaw went over to the corner, took hold of the lath, and lowered it so he could examine the end. Finding nothing there he levered it round, taking care not to hit anything, until he and Willis could study the opposite end. He gave a low murmur of satisfaction and directed the detective-sergeant's attention to a small, deeply-driven hole in the rough wood.

'Penny to a pound that's it,' Willis muttered.

Henshaw brought the bent hairgrip from his pocket and pushed the abraded half into the hole. It fitted exactly, and with a reasonable amount of tightness.

'Let's try the window,' Henshaw murmured, and still watched by the amazed solicitor he went over to it.

Willis, after some difficulty with the stiff catch, got the lower sash up, and Henshaw levered the lath outside. At its fullest stretch it reached the drain, and left a good few feet of length to spare.

'What happens now?' Willis murmured. 'Do we go and examine the drain?'

'Definitely. It'll be a rotten job, but maybe we can get the janitor to give us something to make it a little less messy. Come on.'

As Henshaw withdrew the lath from the window and tugged the bent grip from the end, returning it to his pocket, Minton exploded abruptly.

'What in the blue blazes are you trying to prove *now*, superintendent?'

'Just an angle, sir — and, indirectly it helps you.'

'Hmm. Incidentally, thanks for smashing the window as you did. I've been intending to mention that. I'm going to charge the repair to the police department!'

Henshaw merely shrugged and jerked his head to Willis. They went downstairs together in search of the janitor. From him they secured an old iron ladle and a bucket. Thus equipped they followed the janitor down into the fuel basement and out into the yard by the opened trapdoor. The drain was only a few feet away from this position.

'All right, you needn't stay,' Henshaw told the janitor briefly. 'We may be some little time about this.'

Baxter nodded and went back below. 'I'll leave the trap up so as you can get back.'

Using the iron handle of the ladle as a lever, Henshaw lifted the small-sized cast-iron grid from the drain and put it on one side. Then he peered down at the muddy residue of rainwater below. Plunging the ladle into it he poured it out into the bucket.

'In case you don't know it, sir, Minton is watching us from his office window,' Willis commented presently.

'Let him!' Henshaw responded. 'Incidentally, Willis, it hasn't rained since Barridge died yesterday — so if that key *was* thrown in here it stands a good chance of not having been washed away.'

He stopped talking and for a time there was only the sound of the iron ladle scraping the porcelain of the drain sides, and the bubbling slop of water. Then at last the ladle could take up no more and there remained a grayish, filthy mess in the depths of the cavity. Wrinkling his nose in disgust, Henshaw pulled up his sleeve, lay down on his side, and reached into the hole. For a while he fished about in the repulsive, cloying muck, and then withdrew his slimed hand. In his palm, filmed with ooze and refuse, was a still bright, brassy Yale key.

'Got it!' Willis breathed. 'And by brilliant reasoning on your part, sir!'

'Never mind the compliments, Willis. It wasn't so much good reasoning on my part as the inevitable consequence of my theory.'

Holding the key in his clenched palm, Henshaw left the sergeant to shove back the grid and pour the water back in the drain. Returning through the basement to the janitor's quarters he washed his hands thoroughly, without commenting upon the outcome of his activities — or, for that matter, even referring to the nature of his search. Then, when the bucket and ladle had been returned, he and Willis went into the hall via the janitor's private doorway.

'Slip upstairs and try this key in the lock of Minton's door,' Henshaw instructed, handing it over to Willis. 'We might as well make sure. I'll see you in the car.'

Willis nodded and went hurrying up the bare staircase. Henshaw went out to the car and settled to wait. In a few minutes the detective-sergeant was back.

'It fits okay, sir,' he announced. 'Mr. Minton's expression was worth a good deal as he watched me pop in and out.'

Henshaw grinned momentarily, and then became serious once more.

'From now on, Willis, Minton is about the least important of my interests — that is, beyond proving his alibi to the hilt. What I want you to do is go round to the various ironmongers and toolmakers in Hadlam — there are about five of them, if I remember rightly — and see if you can trace where the key was made and who gave the order. If it can be managed I want the name and — remote chance, perhaps — description of the person concerned. You should be able to put in a good hour's work before the shops close, anyway. Drive me back to the station first.'

Willis nodded and started the car forward through the evening light to headquarters. Here he left the superintendent and then continued on his way to the first of the ironmongers. Thoughtfully, Henshaw returned to his office, with the information from the sergeant-in-charge that nobody had called or telephoned in the interval.

At his desk, Henshaw settled comfortably, and took his notebook from his pocket. Carefully he added further observations . . .

Additional Facts concerning the make-up of William Barridge:
I am now convinced that he opened Minton's office door and rid himself of the duplicate key by dropping it down the drain in the yard outside. I am inclined to believe that — contrary to my first impression — the bent hairgrip was deliberately — yes deliberately — left in the yard to throw suspicion on Jennifer Carr.
It has to be borne in mind that Barridge telephoned Jennifer C. to call upon him almost at the identical time he met his death. He must also have known that at that time the janitor would not have gone to lunch

and would therefore see her arrive and depart — of which fact he would later inform the police.

I do not believe that blame was switched exclusively to Jennifer Carr, but that she was a second choice upon whom suspicion would inevitably fall if the evidence against the first suspect, Minton, fell to pieces.

If I am to serve the ends of justice I must not arrest either Minton or Jennifer Carr. The issue goes very much deeper . . . The fact that a carbon-copy of a blackmail letter was written by Barridge and the original cannot be traced is, I feel sure, only one indication of the kind of mind William Barridge possessed. I shall not rely on my own judgment for this, however, but will check with an expert whose job it is to understand the manifold reactions of the human brain.

The more I consider my own theory, the more sure I become that the answer to most of this puzzle lies in whatever William Barridge sent to *his brother. If only I knew what it could have been, then I might have the authority to ask the Melbourne police to intercept it at the Australian end. As things stand I have no such authority at all. Alas for the limitations which sometimes encumber the police!*

Henshaw put down his pen and contemplated the legal and jurisprudence books in the case on the opposite side of the office, particularly Hamblin Smith's *Psychology of the Criminal* — then he gave a start as the telephone rang. He picked the instrument up. 'Yes?'

'Telegrams' on the line, sir . . . ' The sergeant in the outer office switched the line through, and Henshaw said briefly, 'Okay, miss — fire away.'

'*Direct Cable from Melbourne, Australia — to Henshaw, Superintendent of Police, Hadlam, Great Britain — Informed by landlady of two thirty-six North Elizabeth Street, Melbourne, that Centinel Carr — spelled C-e-n-t-i-n-e-l C-a-r-r, died on the second December, nineteen forty-six. Full details of death — suicide by hanging — will follow by airmail from police department. Believed Carr died through depression and financial stress. Regret unable to give further information. Chief of Police, Melbourne.* Shall I repeat the cable, sir?'

'No thanks, I have it,' Henshaw replied, putting down the receiver as he finished off the shorthand notes he had been making. He smiled slightly to himself, reflected, then picked up the directory. When he had Jennifer Carr's number he had the sergeant get it for him and then sat back in his chair as the woman's pleasant voice floated to him over the line.

'Hello, Mrs. Carr — Superintendent Henshaw here. I thought you might like to know that my assumption that you might be a widow has been justified. I have just received a cable from Australia. Your husband committed suicide by hanging himself, on the second December last year, the very day he wrote to you.'

'Suicide?' the woman's voice whispered. 'Then — then am I right in thinking that

that letter of his was a sort of last will and testament? But why didn't he *say* in the letter that he was going to do that instead of just telling me that he wouldn't contest a divorce action?'

'I can think of only one reason,' Henshaw answered. 'He, perhaps, wasn't fully decided in his own mind at that time whether he would commit suicide or not. In case he didn't decide to take his own life he gave you the chance to get a divorce. If he committed suicide — which he did — you would obviously have no need.'

'But I can't understand why nobody has ever got in touch with me. After all, I *was* his wife. Surely, since he was living under his own name, it would have been possible to have traced me through the emigration authorities?'

'I can only offer a guess, Mrs. Carr,' Henshaw replied. 'All your husband needed when he left this country was his birth certificate. He was not compelled to say whether he had a wife or not — and if he lied about it, the authorities would have been none the wiser. He took a year to leave the country, keeping himself hidden, so that when he did emerge any search for him had died down. Once in Australia, he would call himself a single man, no doubt, and that is why no communication regarding him has reached you. Before long I'll have the full facts of his death. I'll pass them on to you, though you may hear something from Australia before long. The police will have been bound to investigate the circumstances of his life prior to his suicide.'

'I want to find out why he did such a thing. After all, he *was* my husband.'

'Of course,' Henshaw agreed quietly. 'I quite understand.'

'Incidentally,' Jennifer Carr went on, 'I've received an order to attend the inquest in Crayley tomorrow morning. I was intending to ring you up about it. I shan't be — *accused* of anything, shall I?'

'You've nothing to fear, Mrs. Carr. I am going to ask for an adjournment of the inquest until the enquiry into Barridge's death is complete.'

'I see — that's a relief! Thanks,

superintendent . . . Goodbye.'

Henshaw rang off. He felt convinced that the information he wanted concerning Centinel Carr, and which he was pretty sure Barridge had already seen and destroyed, would be evident in the *Melbourne Herald*.

'And five days at least to wait,' he murmured in annoyance. 'I can't cable the *Herald* to cable back the item I want because I don't even know if there is one! That sort of expense just on spec. would upset the Chief no end. Blast!'

He went to the door, told the sergeant to arrange for tea to be sent in, and then he wandered over to the bookshelves. Every one of the books within he had, at various times, read through carefully, chiefly to improve his knowledge for his work; and being trained to use his memory far beyond the average he knew he had seen something somewhere about abnormal powers of smell. And it had been in . . .

'*Psychology of the Criminal*,' he murmured, and took the book from the case. Going over to the desk he turned the book's pages slowly, studying the context. The tea and sandwiches were brought in and he dealt with them absently — then suddenly he alighted on the paragraph he wanted:

> 'Defect of the power of sense perception in any direction is always an indication for very thorough examination. As we have just shown, it may be in itself a predisposing cause of delinquency. Or it may be an indication of general mental deficiency. Some observers have stated that the mentally defective have an abnormally keen sense of smell. If this statement is correct it indicates reversion to a primitive type . . . '

Thoughtfully he picked the book up again and began to study it, munching a sandwich and drinking tea meanwhile.

14

When Detective-sergeant Willis returned to headquarters and at six-thirty, he went straight into his superior's office. He found him absorbed in the *Psychology of the Criminal* and making notes from it at intervals.

'Well, Willis, any luck?' Henshaw put the book to one side and motioned to a chair. 'I've left you some tea and half the sandwiches.'

'Thanks, sir. Yes,' Willis went on, answering the question, 'I've had luck. This Yale key — ' he put it on the desk — 'was made by Sheldon's, the ironmongers in Wesley Street. Since it's a small place, the custom isn't as heavy as a big one, and of course I suppose it's logical that Barridge should choose one of the less-frequented shops.'

'Then it *was* Barridge?' Henshaw asked.

'No doubt of it.' Willis poured himself a

cup of tea. 'The blank is still in the possession of Sheldon and the tag label attached to it bears the name 'Jones'. Obviously Barridge gave a false name to cover up his actions. But Sheldon himself remembered the chap who brought the blank because it was impressed in a chunk of carbolic soap — and, of course, Sheldon had to make his copy from that. The man concerned fits Barridge's description exactly.'

'Good,' Henshaw smiled to himself in quiet triumph.

Willis munched a sandwich for a while, then he asked quietly: 'Just what do you make of it all, sir? What was Barridge's game?'

'The implication, first, of Minton — and if that failed, of Jennifer Carr.'

'Then who killed him? If it wasn't Jennifer or Minton, that leaves only Standish, or the janitor or — very nebulously — maybe Mrs. Barridge . . . '

'I believe I have the solution,' Henshaw answered. 'It's just a matter of verification now. You see . . . '

Henshaw paused and glanced up as the

sergeant-in-charge entered.

'There's a Mr. Tinsley to see you, sir. He says it's important. Connected with Barridge.'

Henshaw straightened up. 'Show him in, by all means.'

With a disappointed glance, Willis got up and took the rest of his tea to a corner; then Gordon Tinsley came in, huge hand extended, a grin splitting his beefy face.

'Glad to know you, superintendent! Tinsley's the name. I'm an estate agent in the town — and one of the best! You must have heard of me.'

'Vaguely,' Henshaw conceded, shaking hands. 'Take a seat, Mr. Tinsley. I understand that you have some information concerning the late Mr. Barridge?'

'I most certainly have! And if you want *my* opinion, you police are too slow to catch cold. You should have made an arrest before this!'

Henshaw smiled grimly. 'Suppose you handle your business, Mr. Tinsley, and I'll handle mine? If you have a statement to make the sergeant will take it down.'

'All right with me — I've come along to

find out if you know that Barridge was leading a double life with Jennifer Carr — the woman who's been mentioned quite a lot in the papers.'

'Oh, Mrs. Carr!' Henshaw nodded slowly. 'How do you know?'

'I don't know, but when a man is so friendly with a woman — and when she isn't his wife, either — as to introduce her to you, as large as life, it makes you think. Made *me* think, anyway — '

'This introduction you speak of. Where did it take place — and to whom?'

'Me, of course!' Tinsley boomed. 'A little while ago I was walking home from the office one evening for a change, just to get a bit of exercise, you know, and I ran smack into Barridge. He had a blonde with him, a real smasher, and he introduced her to me as Mrs. Carr. So, says I, old Barridge is stepping out from that ten-ton truck he's married to, is he? Then I got to thinking that perhaps — '

'He didn't make any attempt to disguise his friendship with Mrs. Carr?'

'Disguise it?' Tinsley gave a bellow of laughter. 'Like hell he did! If anything, he seemed pretty proud of it.'

'From which you deduced, somewhat unreasonably, that Barridge was leading a double life?'

'Unreasonably? It's the only answer, isn't it? Might say the same about Mrs. Carr since she's obviously married. 'Less she's a widow, of course. I don't know about that.'

'Doesn't it occur to you,' Henshaw asked, 'that she might have been a business acquaintance?'

'Business is done in office hours — or should be — not after. Besides, I saw Barridge with her on another occasion, a few days afterwards, only I was on a 'bus that time.'

'None of which proves a double life,' Henshaw stated flatly.

'I think it does — and I'll go on thinking it!' Tinsley's tone had become unpleasant. 'I think he introduced me purposely to let the news get to his wife, then he might have had good reason for getting a divorce from her. She's a lazy lump, anyway: I've seen her. I think, though, that the scheme went wrong and she got tough about it and murdered her husband instead. That's the worst of a woman you can't trust — even granting you can trust any of 'em, which I doubt. Now when it comes to *my* little woman, she does as I tell her and — '

'Is that all you have to tell me, Mr. Tinsley?' Henshaw broke in.

'I thought you'd be interested!'

'As far as the incidents themselves are concerned, I am — but not in the construction you place upon them. You've been misled by what's in the newspapers.'

'I'm a man who thinks for himself!' Tinsley snapped. 'I haven't risen to my present position in this town just through being led. I find out, *I* do, and I still think Barridge was leading a double life. I'll even wager,' he added, narrowing his eyes and leaning across the desk, 'that he had it that badly that he'd taken to sending her presents! Now, what do you think of that?'

'Presents?' Henshaw repeated. 'What sorts of presents do you mean?'

'Well, anyway,' Tinsley went on, smugly satisfied, 'I'll wager that nothing else but an attractive woman would have made old Barridge miss his 'bus and walk about with a parcel instead of getting to the office at the usual time. It takes either love or an earthquake to upset a man with the fixed habits of a Barridge.'

Henshaw straightened up, his gaze bright and hard. Willis turned a pair of sharp eyes and waited expectantly.

'Let me get this straight, Mr. Tinsley,' the superintendent said. 'You saw Mr. Barridge with a parcel, you say? When was this? How long ago?'

'Yesterday morning — Monday,' Tinsley answered. 'I saw him from the top of the 'bus, and so did Jim Brady. He's a stockbroker pal I travel with.'

'Are you convinced it *was* Barridge you saw?'

Tinsley stared. 'Of course I'm convinced! I'd know that little ditherer a mile away. It was Barridge all right — even if he did look a bit like Father Christmas.'

'Father Christmas?' Henshaw frowned. 'What do you mean by that? Because of the parcel he was carrying?'

'No — no, because of the chunk of

cotton-wool on his jaw! I never saw such a lump of stuff in all my life. Now, when *I* cut myself shaving I — '

'Yes, it must have been Barridge all right,' Henshaw interrupted. 'Where was he exactly?'

'In the main street — Radnor Street. As a matter of fact he had just come out of the amusement arcade, and come to think of it, there's no better place to buy a present for a woman. You can get all sorts. And in my opinion — '

'What sort of a parcel was he carrying?'

'A round one. In brown paper. I'll wager it was one of those brass plaques, or a costly plate. Something pretty good, anyway. *Mind* you, I don't *know* it was intended for Mrs. Carr, but I just can't picture old Barridge taking time out from the office for any other reason.'

Henshaw was not listening. He had written, *Coming out of amusement arcade, carrying a circular parcel wrapped in brown paper* on his notepad. Then he looked up again and gave a nod.

'Thanks, Mr. Tinsley. Your information will probably be very useful. Anything else?'

'Not that I know of. Look, do you think I'll get my name in the papers for this? It might do me a bit of good in my business if I'm mentioned as a witness. Especially locally. Nothing like a bit of dirt, you know, to bring 'em running.'

Henshaw considered him coldly and then shrugged.

'I'm a policeman, Mr. Tinsley, not a newspaper editor. If there is nothing more?' Henshaw got to his feet decisively and Tinsley did likewise and shook hands. The superintendent saw him to the door and added, 'Come in tomorrow evening and look through the typewritten copy of your statement, Mr. Tinsley.'

'Right! I'll be here.' And with a nod the noisy estate agent went on his way.

'A round parcel,' Henshaw muttered. 'So *that's* what he sent to Australia! The coincidence is too plain to be missed. He had it before he went to the office, but there was no sign of it anywhere afterwards.'

'Point is, what was it?' Willis asked. 'I can't somehow see him sending a plate, or a plaque, or anything like that to his brother. And we don't even know that he actually got it from the amusement arcade.'

Henshaw glanced at the clock and compressed his lips. 'Too late now to take a look through the arcade. But first thing tomorrow, before we set off for the inquest, we'll be in there to have a look round. By the way, I forgot to tell you that I've received a cable from Australia stating that Centinel Carr committed suicide by hanging on the same day that he wrote to his wife.'

'He did, did he? Then . . . ' Willis sighed. 'Frankly, sir, I'm beginning to lose track of your moves. Is that information of advantage to you, or otherwise?'

'It's confirmation of what I had thought. The actual suicide of Carr does not concern me.'

Henshaw went across to the locker, where he had put the various articles belonging to the Barridge case, and from it lifted the long-bladed knife that had done the deed. He returned to the desk and sat down with the knife balanced between his fingertips, studying it. Then at length he took the knife and balanced it across one finger. 'That's interesting,' he commented. 'Notice where the centre of balance comes?'

It came at the spot where the hilt crosspiece was fixed — in other words, three-quarters of the way along the total length.

'The handle is heavier than the blade, then?' Willis asked.

'Considerably — and it's important, too.' Henshaw came to a decision. 'You finish off whatever typing you have to do, Willis, and then get off home. I'm going over to the forensic department in Crayley. There's something about this knife that I want to be sure of. Tomorrow morning, bright and early, we'll have a look through that amusement arcade — then on to the inquest.'

'Right, sir.'

Willis would have liked to have asked his superior to continue his explanations from the point where they had been interrupted by the infuriating Gordon Tinsley, but there was such concentration on his chief's face he did not press the matter.

With the knife in a protective wrapper, Henshaw drove the distance to Crayley inside fifteen minutes. Since the police headquarters and special departments were open night and day it did not signify that it was well after seven o'clock. The night superintendent in charge of the forensic department greeted him cordially, and Henshaw looked round the emptiness of the laboratory.

'Nobody home?' he enquired.

'Not at this time. Soon get somebody if it's important. What's the trouble?'

Henshaw reflected swiftly. 'Come to think of it I don't need an expert for a job like this. I can do it for myself. I want to examine the hilt of this knife under the most powerful microscope you've got.'

The superintendent nodded to an array of high-powered instruments on a nearby bench. 'Help yourself, Henshaw. Quite welcome.'

'Thanks.' Henshaw took off his uniform-cap, selected the most powerful instrument of all, then settled himself before it and switched on the spot-lighting apparatus. Gently he slid the hilt of the knife under the binocular lenses and adjusted the focus. The smooth gray metal crept from a blur into pin-sharp detail, and what had appeared smooth to the naked eye was now an elongated plain of unexpected roughness, split by several depressions, valleys, and small chasms. In other words, scratches — invisible to the eye.

Henshaw examined every available part of the hilt, and always his attention came back to the chasm-like gouges. In some of them were what appeared to be fine hairs. In actuality they must have been incredibly fine, for they were only just visible even under this intense magnification.

Finally, Henshaw looked across the laboratory. 'Have you a moment, super?' he called. 'I'm a bit out of my depth here.'

'Pleasure.' The superintendent came over and waited.

'On the hilt of this knife there are some scratches, and in them are hairy-like traces clinging to the rough edges of the scratches. I'd like to know what they are, only I seem to have reached the limit of magnification.'

The superintendent looked at the

instrument and smiled. 'Not by a long way,' he said, screwing in a fresh eyepiece. 'I'll soon see if I can help you.'

Henshaw vacated the chair and stood at one side to watch. With a pair of extremely delicate forceps the superintendent removed one or two of the shreds from the scratches and transferred them to a slide, which slide took the place of the knife hilt. Then, changing lenses again until he had the absolute maximum, he studied the 'whiskers' carefully.

'There's so little to go on I can't be certain,' he said finally, 'but I'd say the shreds are wood. There are faint signs of natural graining.'

'What sort of wood is it?'

'Oak. That's one wood which is always distinctive.'

'That's all I need,' Henshaw breathed, picking the knife up and returning it to its wrapper. 'Thanks, super — you've done more for me than you'll ever know.' With a handshake Henshaw took his departure.

Instead of returning to his office he went to Minton's home and was shown into the solicitor's study by the maid.

Then presently Minton himself came in.

'Well, what now?' he asked curtly.

'I want to enter your office, Mr. Minton, and examine it,' Henshaw said. 'That is, your private office. You might let me have the keys — and if you want you can come along with me just to satisfy yourself. It'll be quicker than my wasting time getting the necessary authority to act on my own.'

'No reason why I should come with you,' the solicitor answered, tugging his key ring from his pocket and taking from it the two Yales which opened his own and the main office doors. 'But I'd like some explanation as to why you keep dashing in and out of my office. What's going on?'

'There's good reason for everything I'm doing, Mr. Minton — believe me. And thanks,' Henshaw added, taking the keys and slipping them in his pocket. 'I'll send a constable over with these first thing in the morning or later tonight . . . I take it you haven't heard anything from Chief Inspector Slade yet?'

'No.' Minton gave a heavy smile. 'I shan't run away, though, if that's what you're thinking! I'm far too anxious to see that my alibi is proven.'

'That I know — and it's my guarantee,' Henshaw said. Then he followed behind Minton as the latter showed him to the front door.

'One thing I would like you to promise me,' the solicitor said, and Henshaw hesitated in the porch. 'If I'm arrested — as I fully expect to be — let me know who really *did* kill Barridge. He was such a weak-kneed character that I can't picture him as being dangerous enough to *need* killing!'

'You'll get all the details, sir,' Henshaw promised him.

Henshaw went down the driveway to his car. He drove the car through the busy town to Parkhurst Street, and Minton's office. The outer door was closed, but his thunderous hammerings upon it finally brought the janitor hurrying to open it.

'Oh, it's you, sir!' Baxter shuffled back into the shadows. 'Never expected anybody at this time.'

'The police are liable to go anywhere at *any* time,' Henshaw told him. 'I'm going up to Mr. Minton's office."

Henshaw went up the bare staircase to the first floor, aware that the janitor's eyes were watching him from the gloom of the hall, its intense darkness relieved but slightly by the dim reflected glow from the back regions.

Letting himself into Minton's general office, Henshaw put on the light and went straight across to Minton's room, unlocked it and stepped inside, switching on the light. Standing just in the doorway he remained motionless, surveying — then he went over to the desk.

Satisfying himself that it was solid oak, the same as the tall, ornamental-backed chair, he pushed hard against it — once, twice, but failed to shift it in the slightest. Going down on his knees he examined the thick pile carpet and found that the tremendous weight of the desk had sunk it quite half an inch below the level of the carpet pile and, manifestly, the desk had not been moved for long enough.

'Good!' he murmured — and proceeded to turn his attention to the chair, examining its ornamental back with the whirligig loops, slits, arches, and imitation vineries. It was a beautiful oak chair, a rare specimen.

Thoughtfully, Henshaw took out his spring rule and measured the chair carefully. From the base of the back legs to the top of the back it measured five feet — an unusual length, at least by modern standards. Then he measured it across and determined in inches the dimensions of the loops, slits, and arches. Presently, he seized the chair and rammed it hard against the desk, shoved and pushed and twisted it about, finally desisting with a grim smile.

'The mind of a contortionist,' he muttered, and from his pocket took the knife and slipped it out of its protective cover.

It was at this very moment that a slight sound behind him made him turn. There was a figure in the doorway of the office, watching him.

It was Arthur Standish, the junior clerk.

15

A look of puzzlement and annoyance on his face, the superintendent slipped the knife back in the cover and returned it to his pocket.

'Hello,' Standish greeted calmly, taking off his soft hat. 'Still prowling around, superintendent? I just couldn't think who it could be — all the lights on and everything.'

'What are you doing here?' Henshaw asked shortly.

'Why, I'm here to work, that's all. There's quite a lot of overtime to make up for now, you know — since Mr. Barridge died.'

'I didn't hear you knock on the front door downstairs.'

'Why should I? It was already open. I wondered about it, to tell you the truth. Now I understand. Old Baxter must have left it open in readiness for you to leave.'

'Yes . . . I suppose so.' Henshaw

compressed his lips. 'Overtime, eh?'

'Is anything the matter, superinten-dent?' Standish asked. 'Did I give you a fright, turning up as I did?'

'Of course not . . . You'd better get on with your work, hadn't you — ? And I'll get on with mine.'

'Fair enough,' Standish agreed, shrug-ging; then a faint wonder crossed his gray, uninteresting face. 'But look here — what are you doing? Does the old man know you're playing about in here?'

'I don't have to answer that question, but I will. Yes, he *does* know. Satisfied?'

'All right, all right — I only asked because if he finds anything disturbed in this office he might blame me for it. I've taken Barridge's place now, you see.'

'How on earth can he blame *you* for anything which is disturbed in here? You haven't a key to get in, have you, any more than Barridge had?'

'Well . . . no,' Standish admitted slowly. 'But after what has happened I think the boss has started wondering just how many of us *have* got duplicate keys.'

Henshaw studied the impassive face;

then he came to a decision. He would not proceed with the experiment he had intended. Though he could lock Standish out of the office, the very fact that the fellow was even present put him off his stroke.

'I've nothing more I need to do here,' he said briefly. 'I'll leave you to your overtime.'

'Okay — and I'm sorry if I disturbed you.'

Henshaw led the way out of the room, closed the door after Standish had followed him, and then left the enquiry office without another word.

'Nothing wrong with overtime, I suppose, especially with Barridge dead,' he muttered, getting into his car. 'But I don't like that fellow Standish! Too sly. All the same I can't see how he can upset my notions.'

He drove out of Parkhurst Street into the main road, and so, finally, to his headquarters. The sergeant informed him that Willis had just departed for home.

'All right,' Henshaw responded, 'and

don't disturb me for the next ten minutes unless it's absolutely essential. I've some thinking to do.'

He found the statements of all parties concerned neatly typed, clipped together, and placed on the desk. Laying them on one side he sat down, bringing the knife out of his pocket. With his spring rule he measured the width of the hilt and then referred to the various figures he had made in Minton's office.

He glanced at the clock, realized there was little more he could do on this particular evening, and recalled that his wife had promised a steak pie for when he got home. All of a sudden the problem of William Barridge meant less than nothing. It was time to relax, to allow his subconscious mind to go to work while he occupied his active mind with a complete diversion . . .

★　★　★

Henshaw was back in the office at quarter to nine the following morning to discover that Willis had already arrived and was waiting for him, apparently in an eager mood.

''Morning, sir,' he greeted his superior, as he came in. 'I made enquiry on my way down, just to be sure, and verified that the amusement arcade opens at nine ... I've been trying to imagine what it could be, of circular shape, which Barridge sent to Australia — but without result.'

'We'll go and have a look round, anyway,' Henshaw said. 'Come along — we'll walk. It isn't so far.'

Together they left the office and as they strode along briskly in the keen morning air Willis raised a question.

'Last night, sir, when you left the station, you took the knife with you to the forensic department in Crayley. Did you find out what you wanted?'

'I did, yes - - namely, that the knife hilt is badly scratched and there are faint traces of wood fibre — oak to be exact — clinging inside the rough edges of the scratches.'

'Proving what?' Willis gave a frown.

'Proving the point which has been

worrying the Chief quite a deal — how the knife had only Minton's fingerprints and nobody else's.'

'Do you mean by that that nobody *did* hold it — that Minton's fingerprints were already on it from normal usage and were not disturbed in the process of killing Barridge?'

'That's exactly what I mean,' Henshaw agreed. 'The scratches were not enough to obliterate the fingerprints entirely, of course ... Last night I was going to experiment with the knife for myself when I was interrupted by the arrival of Standish — '

'Standish!' Willis gave an amazed glance.

'He'd come back to put in some overtime — or so he said. Anyway, his arrival upset my plans and I couldn't try out my idea as I'd intended. But I have made measurements, and one of the many slits in the ornamental designing of that chair in Minton's office is of exactly the same width — or a shade larger — than the hilt of the knife. Add to that the fact that the knife is heavier in the hilt than the blade, and what do you get?'

'That the knife was balanced in a slit of the chair back, point outwards?'

'Correct,' Henshaw assented. 'To that add the fact that the chair is very solid, and the desk against which it stands even more so. Nothing short of a battering ram would move the desk, nor the chair either when wedged against it.'

As he and Henshaw neared the right-angled street which led towards the amusement arcade Willis spoke again.

'Are you suggesting, sir, that somebody forced Barridge to step backwards — or something like it — so that he collided with the knife projecting out of the chair ornamentation? I can't quite see that. Too chancy. One step to right or left and he'd have missed it.'

'But he *didn't* miss,' Henshaw pointed out, with a dry smile. 'And if you think hard enough you ought to see why. Anyway, here's the arcade. Let's see what it has to tell us.'

It had only just opened, and they both had to hang about for a while before the various stalls and stores began to open up. Though the arcade was actually a connection between two ends of a street, it would have been more correct to designate it as a market. There were food stores, haberdashery stores, hardware stores, bookstalls, jewellery counters — all lumped together with a scattering of gambling machines in the shape of small-sized pin tables, racing games, roller-ball, and similar gadgets.

The two men considered the machines as the stalls began to open. 'I don't think there is much among those which would account for a round, circular parcel, sir,' Willis commented. 'And even if you win anything out of them, it's only cheap stuff — certainly not worth a registered parcel to Melbourne!'

With the stalls beginning to open the sideshow department was also showing signs of stirring into life. Shutters were being taken down and offerings like Aunt Sally and Hell's Kitchen came into view.

'A plate from Hell's Kitchen?' Willis suggested — then he shook his head over the impossibility of it.

They wandered first to the cooked meats counter and considered the prospect of some round, flat tins containing pork — then the illogical idea of a half-starved country sending food to a much better stocked one became evident, and they moved on.

At a store containing *bric-a-brac* and so-called *objets-d'art* they lingered again, and Henshaw even opened a discussion with the aged, highly refined proprietor over the possibility of Barridge having purchased one of the flat, ancient shields which hung in pairs — chiefly for ornamentation — on the back wall.

But it seemed that no man of Barridge's description had ever been near the store.

Henshaw then continued on his way with Willis beside him. They paused next at a fancy goods stall and discovered all kinds of things that were circular, but nothing as far as they could judge which would have appeal for a successful engineer. Besides, most of the articles were designed to catch the feminine eye. Nor had the proprietor any remembrance of serving a man of William Barridge's description.

Increasingly morose, and glancing to either side of them, they pursued a course to the opposite end of the arcade.

'Get your voice recorded, sir?' suggested a hoarse voice. 'Be a bit of a surprise for the wife.'

'No, thanks,' Henshaw answered dryly. 'She hears quite enough of it as it is.'

He glanced briefly at the red-faced proprietor leaning round a booth like a telephone-box, and then walked on pensively. But all of a sudden he stopped and swung round. In fact, he did it so abruptly the proprietor started.

'*What* did you say?' Henshaw demanded.

'Eh? I — I said get your voice recorded.' The man spread his hands and looked apologetic. 'Sorry I bothered you, superintendent. I suppose you're on duty, seeing as you've got your uniform on. I was only trying to get some business. It's precious bad in the winter.'

Henshaw took a swift survey of the affair like a telephone-box. Now he came to look at it properly he saw that crimson letters on a white background exhorted the populace to hear themselves speak.

'You mean this is one of those places where you can record your own voice?' Henshaw asked sharply. 'That it?'

'That's it — on the Massaner System. It makes the record while you talk. All automatic and private. Nobody can hear you. And you can even play it back to yourself if you want.'

'A round parcel,' Willis murmured, a glint in his eye. 'A record!'

'That's it,' Henshaw agreed. 'I could kick myself for not thinking of it sooner. I want some information,' Henshaw added, turning to the man again. 'Official information, I mean. Can you remember if, on Monday morning, early on, a smallish man with a chunk of cotton-wool on his jaw made a record here?'

'Thin-faced feller? Meek and mild sort?'

'That's him.'

'Yes — sure he did. I remember him particularly by that cotton wool stuck on his face. What about him?'

'Did he give his name?'

'He'd no need to. So long as he paid me for making the record that was all I worried about.'

'You are quite sure that the record can be made in absolute privacy?' Henshaw insisted.

'Certainly it can!' The man looked transiently indignant, 'You simply go in, switch on the power, speak into the microphone, and a red light goes up when the record is near its end. You switch off and take the record from under the tracking needle. That's all there is to it. It's there right in front of you, and you can watch it work.'

'I see — by which means there is no master-record or anything left?'

'None at all. You only need a master-record when you make hundreds of recordings from one original — like a gramophone company. The person who makes the record is the only one who knows what's on it — 'cept those who hear it afterwards, of course.'

'Which can be played on an ordinary gramophone, I suppose?'

'Yes — a soft needle for preference.

Naturally, the recording isn't what you'd call terrific, but you don't expect it at the price.'

Henshaw motioned. 'I'd like to see it work. Show me, will you?'

'Pleasure.' With a nod the proprietor moved into the inside of the sound-recording booth and performed the actions he had previously described.

He switched on the power, gently lowered the tracking arm and needle on to a blank record spinning on a silent turntable. Then he talked some gibberish into the microphone hanging in front of him. Switching off, he transferred the record to a normal electric sound-reproducer. From the amplifier his own words came back, suffering from a good deal of 'woof' and tinniness but distinct enough just the same.

'That's marvelous!' Henshaw declared. 'Not just the apparatus, I don't mean — but the implication behind it. Thanks! Very much obliged to you.'

He turned away and, Willis at his side, made for the exit.

'Of course,' the detective-sergeant said,

'there's no doubt but what it must have been a record which Barridge sent to his brother — but what was *on* it? Greetings? A birthday wish? Or something?'

'I'll stake everything I've got,' Henshaw replied, 'that that record contains, in Barridge's own voice, the answer to everything we want to know.'

'Then — he must have known of the crime before it happened?'

'Of course he did, because he *made* the crime happen. Don't bother me now, though, Willis, I've other things to think about.'

Willis nodded, and thereafter did his best to puzzle things out in his own mind. When he and the detective-sergeant had returned to headquarters he had to come out of his reverie for in the office was a broad-shouldered figure in a raglan overcoat, a soft hat pushed up on his forehead.

'Slade!' Henshaw exclaimed, delighted, shaking the man's hand as he got up.

Chief Inspector Slade of Scotland Yard's C.I.D. was an expressionless man whose square face was only saved from downright melancholy by a twinkle in the blue eyes. He looked — and was — the kind of man who could absorb any shock without betraying the vestige of a reaction.

'Good to see you again, Henshaw,' he greeted. 'And you, Willis. Always glad to see two young chaps getting on.' He resumed his seat and Henshaw and Willis sat down. 'I've come over to deal with Minton,' he explained. 'We tidied up the other three in London yesterday, following your 'phone call.'

'Then there was enough evidence?' Henshaw questioned.

'Evidence! We've had that for long enough: the only reason we didn't act was because we were waiting for one or other of them to make a mistake and so make it easier for us to step in. Now one of them *has* made a mistake — Minton. You can congratulate yourself, Henshaw,' Slade added. 'Four doubtful members of society nailed at one swoop, and purely at your instigation.'

'Nice to know, but that doesn't really interest me,' the superintendent replied, smiling. 'What about Minton? Is his alibi right? Did any of those men speak?'

'They spoke, all right,' Slade confirmed. 'Once they knew that it was because of Minton that we'd nabbed them they didn't pull their punches one bit in saying that he was one of them. You can take it for granted, Henshaw — Minton's alibi is correct . . . And I hope,' Slade added, 'that it doesn't make things difficult for you in this Barridge business.'

'Not at all. His elimination as a suspect is what I expected. Incidentally, when you arrest him you might as well have Willis with you. I want Minton to sign the statements he'd made to me before you wheel him off.'

'Okay . . . ' Slade's humorous blue eyes twinkled. 'You know me well enough by now, Henshaw, to know that I've no wish to steal your thunder — but if, as an old hand at the game, I can give you any help just say so. Be only too glad.'

'I appreciate that,' Henshaw smiled. 'Yesterday, or Monday, I might have been glad of it because I started to run off up the wrong street — then, remembering you once saying that it's the *mind* of a man which matters more than anything else in the world, I stopped and reflected. Then I about-faced and worked from a totally new angle. Because of that I'm inclined to think, barring a few points which have yet to be verified, that I have the whole case solved.'

'Splendid!' Slade looked genuinely pleased, and for that matter he was. The success of a junior official, particularly if he worked to methods that he himself had suggested at some time, was something that pleased him.

'There's just one thing,' Henshaw said, after a pause. 'And I think maybe you can help me . . . I'd like to see a psychiatrist.'

'A psychiatrist! Great Scot, don't tell me the case has strained you to *that* extent!'

'No,' Henshaw smiled. 'It's just that I want to verify some conclusions I've formed, mainly from Smith's *Psychology of the Criminal*, and the only person who can help me is an expert on the mind. We have none in Hadlam whom I'd care to approach, but in London you have the pick. Anybody you can recommend?'

True to his code of never interfering in another official's business, Slade asked no questions as to the why or wherefore.

'You might try Frank Butler of Harley Street,' he said finally. 'He's one of the best men I know at brain-picking. Helped me out with several cases. Mention my name and he'll see you quickly enough, otherwise he's a bit difficult to approach. In fact,' Slade added, reaching out to the telephone, 'I'll give him a ring and tell him you're coming. When will it be?'

'Later on today sometime, and — Good lord!' Henshaw jumped to his feet hurriedly as he caught a glimpse of the clock. 'Will you excuse me, Slade? I've an inquest to attend in Crayley and I'd clean forgotten all about the darned thing. Willis will have to come, too. Look, I must get that statement signed by Minton before he — '

'Don't excite yourself,' Slade said, when he had asked for Frank Butler's number. 'I've a man with me. He's having some breakfast in the town at the moment. I'll take the statement and get it signed, then return it here. Rely on it. Now get off to that inquest. Coroners are touchy blighters sometimes.'

'Thanks,' Henshaw responded gratefully. 'See you again.'

* * *

As he had intended from the first, Henshaw obtained an adjournment of the inquest, then he and Willis returned to headquarters towards lunchtime, to find that Chief Inspector Slade had kept his word and, presumably, 'attended' to Minton. His statement, duly signed, was in the exact centre of the blotter.

'You'd better take these others round and get them signed,' Henshaw said, glancing at the detective-sergeant. 'I want to be left alone for a bit to work out what I'm going to ask Butler, then I'll be going on to London.'

'See you again then, sir,' Willis said, and picking up the statements that still needed signing, he left the office.

Henshaw took out his notes and went

through them, then on a separate sheet of paper he began to write a whole series of statements. Gradually a list began to take shape:

1. *Dealings with a bookmaker that were entirely mythical.*
2. *Exceptionally keen sense of smell.*
3. *Worshipped highly successful brother.*
4. *Reticent, very retiring, yet never once forgetting a slight or an insult.*
5. *Always being bullied as a boy, held in contempt by his employer and the staff, and even by his wife and children.*
6. *Had developed endocarditis and took no steps to arrest its progress.*
7. *Slighted, cuttingly so, by Jennifer Carr.*
8. *Studied anatomy.*
9. *Recorded his own voice.*
Side Issues (but relevant)
Made a will that cannot be found.
Had a suicide clause inserted in his insurance policy at approximately the time he met Jennifer Carr.

Went out of his way to be seen with Jennifer Carr.

Henshaw put down the pen and smiled reflectively to himself. He picked up the railway guide and studied it, finding he had just twenty minutes in which to change into mufti and get the London train.

16

When Henshaw got to the office the next morning he found Willis there to greet him.

'Any luck in London, sir?' he asked.

'All the luck I could have wished for.' Henshaw rubbed his palms together in satisfaction. 'This business is finished with, Willis — or will be when we get verification in the shape of that record Barridge made.'

'You saw that chap Butler, then? The psychiatrist?'

'Yes — and got his professional answers to a lot of questions which had been puzzling me.'

Henshaw went over to his desk and glanced at the memo. pad. 'So the Chief called last night, did he?'

'That's right, sir. He said he'd look in first thing this morning. Be here any moment, I expect.'

He had hardly finished speaking before the sergeant-in-charge knocked and came in, only it was not to announce the Chief Constable but to hand in a sealed letter with the official stamp of Crayley Police Headquarters upon it.

Henshaw tore the flap of the big envelope and from it took Jennifer Carr's three letters. With them was a brief note from the superintendent of the forensic department. With a musing smile Henshaw read:

Crayley Police Headquarters.
Dear Henshaw,
There doesn't seem to be much point in our retaining these letters any longer. Careful tests have been made of them at intervals with our instruments, and the experts are of opinion that, if we were to wait until Doomsday the ink would not become any darker. It has already reached maximum. This means the letters were originally written at least two years ago, and maybe long before that.
Hope this helps,
Bob.
(Robert Baines, Superintendent.)

'Couldn't be better,' Henshaw murmured, handing the note over to Willis. He read it through, then said:

'Then Mrs. Carr has been telling the truth all along? She said two years ago at least. Then what was Barridge doing with them in his drawer with the tops — addresses — cut off?'

'Deflecting guilt on to Jennifer, as he had been doing in so many instances.'

The arrival of the Chief Constable stopped Henshaw from going any further. He greeted the Colonel amiably and motioned to a chair.

'Missed you last night,' Wilton said, sitting down. 'What took you to London?'

'The need to verify certain conclusions, sir, which only a psychiatrist could handle. Chief Inspector Slade was good enough to fix things up for me with Dr. Butler.'

'Butler, eh?' The Colonel reflected and lighted his pipe. 'Mmm — a good man. But why did you want him?' Then before Henshaw could answer the Chief Constable went on: 'The days are flying past, Henshaw. Judging from your reports,

334

you've spent a lot of time sorting out every intricate little detail without arriving at anything definite. I'm hoping you'll tell me whom you're going to arrest.'

'You did say you'd give me a week or two to sort it out, sir. There are two more things to get yet — a parcel and a newspaper, both from Australia. I can't see the parcel getting here before another six weeks have gone. I certainly don't think it will be airmailed, as the newspaper will.'

'You mean that we have to wait that long before we can arrest Barridge's murderer? I don't like it, Henshaw — damned if I do.'

'Nobody is guilty of the murder of Barridge,' Henshaw answered quietly. 'He was a suicide.'

The Chief Constable drew hard at his pipe. 'Oh, come now, Henshaw! Stabbed in the back! We discussed that and — '

'The stabbing in the back is only one aspect of a remarkably ingenious scheme, sir. Stabbing in the back made it *look* like murder, but the fact remains that it was *not* murder. Barridge killed himself because, dead, and as the chief figure in a murder drama, he knew he would at least have the spotlight, even though it was posthumous.'

'Then he must have been mad!'

'In a sense, he was.' Henshaw sat back in his chair. 'That is one reason why I went to see a psychiatrist, to verify my conclusions. Barridge was not mad in the accepted sense of the term: he was a victim of repression. Without using the technical jargon of a brain-specialist, a victim of repression — that is, a person crushed continually since babyhood, bullied, and generally being a mug for everybody — develops what is called a 'repression complex' . . . '

Henshaw paused and took a note from his wallet. 'I have the facts here, sir, as Dr. Butler gave them to me. 'This repressed complex is not killed by being forced into the subconscious: it is merely dormant, but it often happens that it escapes into the normal consciousness, and for a time, dominates the person completely. In turn, that produces the well-known characteristic of egomania, which is distinct from a psychopath in that a psychopath usually has the urge to slay somebody else, whereas the egomaniac is interested in only one thing — drawing attention to himself, or herself, no matter what the cost. It is as if all the longing for attention which had not been gratified throughout life suddenly welled up to the surface in William Barridge and demanded satisfaction.'

The Colonel had become absorbed in thought, heedless that his pipe had gone out.

'At first,' Henshaw went on, 'I arrived at the conclusion that it was straightforward murder. The first clue I got pointing in the opposite direction was that an examination of the dirt under Barridge's fingernails showed he had never struggled with anybody prior to his death — directly contrary to the evidence of a struggle in Minton's office. Clearly, then, it began to look as though the signs of a struggle had been *arranged*. By whom? Apparently Barridge.

'Suspecting now that he was a suicide, I got to know all I could about him.

Everything suggested the touch of an egomaniac. Having always been considered meek and mild, he set out to prove himself the opposite. There were betting-cards pointing to him being a gambler, which I proved he was not, though where he got the betting-cards I don't know. He showed himself in the company of an attractive woman — actually for a double reason, but principally to show that he could kick over the traces and be utterly immoral. To add to this he had what purported to be passionate love letters written exclusively to him.'

'And you believe that a man suffering from egomania *would* do all these things?' the Chief Constable questioned.

'Psychiatry says it is so, and that's good enough for me, sir. Conduct is the direct result of mental life. At one fell swoop Barridge turned everything to his own advantage — but I was disturbed, until recently, by a missing, vital factor. Though convinced that he was an egomaniac I knew there must be sign of its consummation somewhere, some *ending* to the plan. In this, Butler agreed with me. It was essential to Barridge that he have the last laugh in some manner. Proof must be laid somewhere wherein he would explain how completely he had fooled everybody and proved himself the perpetrator of a perfect crime. Proof is usually to be found, with such egomaniacs, in a diary or a letter. I couldn't find anything like that. Then I discovered that Barridge had recorded his voice — and I'm as sure as that record will contain his confession, thereby rounding off the whole scheme. Triumph, in other words, for him — even though he is no longer alive to enjoy the sensation.'

'Well,' Wilton said, musing, 'that would certainly seem to explain the psychiatric angle of the business, but what about the mechanics of the crime . . . ? Incidentally, how did Barridge's abnormal sense of smell fit in?'

'It is a common failing — or gift — of a person of twisted mentality, so Butler assured me. However, as to the mechanics of the crime. I think Barridge lost interest in living when he knew he had endocarditis. True, the disease could have been checked, but from his point of view where was the point in prolonging his life? He would still remain browbeaten, insignificant. His brooding over this did a good deal to bring on the sudden urge of egomania, which decided him to have a last fling. And this last fling came about, apparently, through a combination of circumstances.

'He was getting the *Melbourne Herald* regularly from his brother — and incidentally his hero-worship of his successful brother showed again his complex — and I incline to the view that in the still missing issue of the *Herald* there was an account of the suicide and circumstances surrounding Centinel Carr. It is possible that, feeling depressed himself and inclined to take his own life, the account aroused a morbid interest in Barridge. It's also possible he remembered it clearly for this reason, and also because of the unusual name of 'Centinel'. Barridge could hardly have read of this before Mrs. Carr, wife of Centinel, walked into the office to sue for divorce. Since her husband wrote to her only a week before the announcement of his death in the paper the times would almost synchronize.'

Henshaw tapped the desk for emphasis.

'Imagine Barridge's feelings! He was already considering taking his own life and casting round for a 'grand slam'. He must have gathered from Mrs. Carr's conversation that she had love letters from her husband and he knew that the Centinel Carr, of whom he had read, must be the same person. Hence he had no need to pursue divorce proceedings but could arrange matters to suit himself. He did not ask for love letters as such, but Mrs. Carr turned them over to him just the same. Knowing — again perhaps from her conversation — that there were no dates and no name to whom they were addressed, 'Snookums' taking its place, he could easily make it look as though they had been sent to him by cutting off the addresses. That, I think, is what he did, convincing Mrs. Carr that Minton himself would not be interested until the preliminaries were settled. Just prior to this arrangement I think Barridge had made advances to Mrs. Carr — and *meant* them — being desperately anxious to find somebody who would take some interest in him. Her complete rejection of him stung his ego and he resolved that Mrs. Carr, like Minton, should be suspected of murder, and perhaps even be executed for it.'

The Chief Constable stirred a little in his chair and relit his pipe.

'Naturally,' Henshaw resumed, 'only Barridge's own confession can prove me right or wrong. His idea was, I think, to make Minton the chief suspect — and how he hated Minton! In this he was nearly successful. Barridge must have known that Minton was a black marketeer, just as he must have known in advance that Minton was going to a Black Market meeting in London when he was supposed to be going to Liverpool. That is why Barridge took that day for his 'perfect' crime. Knowing Minton would be with Black Market associates he knew, too, that he wouldn't be able to form an alibi for himself without divulging his activities. It was a two-way trap — and it worked. Barridge knew that with Minton having the only key to the office it would make him extra suspect, and for good measure he added, among his own effects, a carbon-copy of a blackmailing letter — the original of which was presumably destroyed — which provided a beautiful motive for Minton desiring to commit murder. As for the knife, the prints were already on it. All Barridge had to do was use the knife without disturbing the prints. He arranged the office to look as though there had been a struggle, rid himself of the duplicate key through the window, and then killed himself.'

'How does Mrs. Carr also become an object of his venom?' Wilton questioned.

'Three people were the intended victims,' Henshaw replied. 'Minton came first, Mrs. Carr second — the evidence against her being a hairgrip of the type she uses and also through a brooch she must have dropped accidentally, and which Barridge turned to account later. In regard to Mrs. Carr, he knew the love letters would be found, and there being no files of a divorce case, he guessed the police would think she was lying. Further, he 'phoned to her — on an untraceable dial system — so she would be in the vicinity at the time he met his death. Of course, Barridge must have known his scheme to involve her had holes in it — namely, how did she get in Minton's locked office? Why were her fingerprints not on the knife, and so on? But he did, at least, reckon that the mess she would get into would be ample repayment for the way she had slighted him. And when it came out that her husband had committed suicide the law would be entitled to ask why she had started divorce proceedings that were not necessary. She could deny having received the facts from Australia, but only her word for it would not be considered sufficient. It would look as though she got into touch with Barridge solely to make love to him — and then kill him — '

'When you said he had the mind of a contortionist you weren't far wrong,' the Chief Constable commented. 'I suppose, then, that his deliberate efforts to be seen with Mrs. Carr — introducing her when he happened on an acquaintance — was to bolster up the idea that he was — er — well, intimate with her?'

'Of course. You may be sure that Barridge had everything worked out to the last detail — which is another peculiar genius that attaches to the egomaniac. Such a person will go through the most ingenious plotting just as long as it draws attention to himself. At root it is self-centredness gone mad.'

'You mentioned a third victim?'

'Mrs. Barridge. He loathed her, too — and if anything convinced me of the suicide theory it was the clause he had inserted in his insurance about the time he met Jennifer Carr. He knew that the money would not be paid to his wife in the event of his suicide. At first, if it was considered to be murder, she would be paid, of course — after the trial. But upon the arrival of his confession — which I am sure will come — Mrs. Barridge would be compelled somehow to refund the amount. Certainly it would embarrass her tremendously. It was a vicious, cunning trick and a last grand slap at his wife. That, I think, is how he outlined his scheme, but — as always happens with a weaver of a perfect crime — parts came unstuck. Science beat him in the fingernail evidence belying the theory of a struggle; Gordon Tinsley beat him unexpectedly by noticing him carrying a circular parcel on Monday morning; he beat himself by being too careful in that he shut *all* the office doors before killing himself. He had not the slightest reason to shut his *own* office door. In that he overstepped himself — '

'And just how did he kill himself?' the Chief Constable asked at length.

'He placed the knife hilt in a slot in the back of the chair in Minton's office so that it was balanced at right angles. He deliberately walked backwards into the blade and the chair and desk were heavy enough to support the impact of his body. The wide hilt crosspiece prevented the knife from slipping backwards into the slot. My measurements of the chair showed that with the knife in the topmost slot it would strike Barridge — he being five feet seven — just below the shoulder.

What led me to this theory was the fact that the blade had entered horizontally. It suggested a mechanical effect. Added to that was the pull of the wound-lip to one side. The chair we found overturned. I think that when Barridge died he fell sideways, not frontwards as he'd calculated, which would have drawn the knife neatly out of the slot and left it embedded in his back. The knife, in dislodging from the chair slot, was momentarily held by it and pulled the chair over, *also* dragging the lip-wound to one side.'

'How could he be sure that he'd hit himself in the right place?' Wilton questioned.

'He studied an anatomy book, which contains many plates of the human body, and since he had a second key he had ample chance to rehearse the effect when he was alone. He knew absolutely what he was up to, and maybe even considered that he was a man of courage. His wife told me that on one occasion he told her that committing suicide demands great courage, and it wasn't just so as to annoy her that he said it.'

'In other words . . . ' The Chief Constable looked at his pipe thoughtfully. 'In other words, Minton and Mrs. Carr were both framed in guilt, eh? He reasoned that by the time his precious confession arrived back from Australia, one or other of them would have paid the price for murdering him — or at the very lowest estimate that Minton would be in jail for black marketing — which he is — and Mrs. Carr perhaps imprisoned or something.'

Henshaw nodded. 'I'm sure he hoped for something like that. With the spotlight on him all the time! As a dead man he achieved a little cheap notoriety: as a living one he achieved exactly nothing. Instead of being man enough to fight back he chose one of the most cowardly ways of getting his own back that I've yet come across. As for that recorded confession of his, it obviously won't be addressed to Scotland Yard, or even to me, for fear of exciting the brother's suspicions, and also it won't be sent airmail when delay is the very essence of the scheme. So, we just have to wait

— for the final details.'

The Chief Constable's manner had changed completely. 'Wait all you have to, Henshaw, but I think you should cable the Melbourne police to intercept that parcel when it arrives and have it sent back airmail. I'll take the responsibility.'

'Right you are, sir. I'll do that.'

★   ★   ★

It was a week later when the *Melbourne Herald* arrived by airmail for Henshaw. The moment he arrived in the office and found it on his desk he tore the wrapper off and spread the newspaper out, Willis watching eagerly at his side. It was not long before they came upon a column in the centre pages headed:

IMMIGRANT'S SUICIDE
An immigrant to this country from Britain, Centinel Carr, was found hanged in his rooms today in the Elizabeth Street area. His landlady made the discovery and called the police. An inquest will be held

shortly. The theory of foul play is discounted by the authorities. According to the landlady Carr was worried financially and depressed in regard to his future in the country he had adopted.

'In other words, just plain depression and the coward's way out,' Henshaw commented, looking up. 'Barridge read it, and you know how I worked out the rest. Realizing that somebody might find the paper containing the announcement of Carr's death he destroyed it. It drew more attention than if he'd left it as it was! I must let the Chief know about this right away and send a copy of it to Mrs. Carr.'

As it transpired, however, later in the day, Jennifer Carr knew of the facts, the Melbourne police having traced her through devious sources as being the widow of Centinel Carr, and information was requested by airmail for the police records.

Henshaw was only scantily interested: his concern was entirely for the safe arrival of the record which would prove or disprove his theories — and the four weeks that had to elapse before the record finally arrived he found the most nerve-racking he had ever experienced.

'Addressed to his wife,' he said, as he studied the label. 'Sent back to us by airmail with the help of the Melbourne police and with James Barridge's permission. Give the Chief a ring, will you, Willis? He'd better come over and hear this for himself . . . ' Willis nodded and turned to the telephone.

Unwrapping the carefully-packed parcel, Henshaw found a handwritten note —

To my dear wife. Just a little surprise

With a grim smile Henshaw took the cheap disc over to the portable gramophone he had brought from home especially for the purpose. He waited until Willis had finished telephoning the Colonel — and obtained his assurance that he would be over right away — and then lowered the needle into the outermost groove.

'Hello, my darling, this is William!' The

voice of Barridge croaking forth, speaking from beyond the grave. 'If you have collected the insurance money for my murder, my dear, you'd better hand it back because I wasn't murdered! I committed suicide! Nobody will ever find out how it was done, but it was. Surprising what you can do when you study anatomy. By now I hope that pig Minton has swung for it — or else Jennifer Carr.

'How am I going to plan to kill myself and make it look like murder? Why should I tell the police how to do their job? The only thing I'm interested in is proving that I'm not such a dithering fool as you thought — as others thought — as *everybody thought*! It takes courage to kill yourself, my dear. Remember me telling you? By the way, if you find evidence that makes me look like a betting man, it's all wrong. I'm not. Gordon Tinsley, a pal of mine, gave me the betting cards last year, and I'm going to use 'em to puzzle the brains of the police, if they've got any! Everything is worked out, even to a brooch belonging to Jennifer Carr.

'Let me get back to the present moment. It is Monday morning, the third of February, nineteen forty-seven, and I am William Barridge. I once made a will, but you'll never find it. If you think I'd ever do you or those infernal kids of ours a good turn, you're vastly mistaken! When this record is played over to the police they will realize that they have been utterly and completely fooled — and by me, the one you considered to be a congenital idiot. I'll bet the papers become full of it, and my only regret is that I shan't be able to see them — but at least this is some consolation. This is going to be one case where the police will see that a clever man can force a miscarriage of justice and make others smart as I've smarted. But I'll have to stop. The record is nearly ended. Goodbye, my dear — and go to the devil!'

'He doesn't admit one detail of what you've proved, sir,' Willis commented.

'He doesn't need to, Willis. I'm right, because every part fits in.'

We do hope that you have enjoyed reading this large print book.

Did you know that all of our titles are available for purchase?

We publish a wide range of high quality large print books including:
Romances, Mysteries, Classics
General Fiction
Non Fiction and Westerns

Special interest titles available in large print are:
The Little Oxford Dictionary
Music Book, Song Book
Hymn Book, Service Book

Also available from us courtesy of Oxford University Press:
Young Readers' Dictionary
(large print edition)
Young Readers' Thesaurus
(large print edition)

For further information or a free brochure, please contact us at:
Ulverscroft Large Print Books Ltd.,
The Green, Bradgate Road, Anstey,
Leicester, LE7 7FU, England.
Tel: (00 44) **0116 236 4325**
Fax: (00 44) **0116 234 0205**